ON THE EDGE OF FEAR

Peter Neeves

Published by New Generation Publishing in 2014

Copyright © Peter Neeves 2014

First Edition

The author asserts the moral right under the Copyright, Designs and Patents Act 1988 to be identified as the author of this work.

ISBN 978-1-78507-186-7

All Rights reserved. No part of this publication may be reproduced, stored in a retrieval system or transmitted, in any form or by any means without the prior consent of the author, nor be otherwise circulated in any form of binding or cover other than that which it is published and without a similar condition being imposed on the subsequent purchaser.

www.newgeneration-publishing.com

New Generation Publishing

Chapter One

Susan lived in a ground floor flat in the suburbs of south London. She shared the flat with her best friend Kathy.

She was sitting in the small lounge reflecting on her recent decisions. What have I done, she thought to herself. Two months ago I had a good job with a regular salary, now I am off to Africa. What have I done?

When she had told her parents she had quit her job they were surprised to say the least but when she had told them she was off to Africa for over five months she could sense that they had thought she had flipped. Her father was enthusiastic about the trip but her mother?

She recalled the recent events; September 12th – resigned from job, September 19th – her 31st birthday, September 20th – booked an overland tour to Africa. She considered each date in turn. Her job in the bank had been fine but after more than 12 years, (she had joined straight from school in 1974) she felt she was getting in a rut. Little chance of promotion and the attitude of her superiors that customers should be sold products they had no real need of just to keep the figures up was something she did not agree with. She didn't like the way things were changing in the profession. Her birthday had been great but she always felt something was missing on these occasions. Or rather someone, as she had never met anyone who would be that special person in whom she could trust and settle down with, get married maybe and have a family. She sighed.

Then she had booked the Africa trip. Probably the effects of too much alcohol from the night before she mused but she knew that weren't true. She was up for an adventure. The brochure, picked up at last year's travel show in Earls Court, had tempted her with trips crossing the Sahara, through the jungles, going on safari; so she had gone to the travel agent in Twickenham, booked the tour that covered all three and a lot more besides, and paid for it there and then. She looked forward to the tour and yet dreaded it. Five months sleeping in a tent. She had never even camped before and hoped she would enjoy it.

The first item she had bought for the trip had been a sleeping bag. She had purchased a comfy looking bag but on getting it home had found that it was far too bulky. This early disaster had made her full of self-doubt and tears of despair had engulfed her. Luckily her flat mate had come to the rescue and had changed it for a more compact and practical one of cotton filled with down. Further purchases had acquired a backpack, an inner sheet, a water container, a money belt and a good camera with plenty of film. Then it was off to the medical centre for countless vaccinations for yellow fever, typhoid, cholera, hepatitis A, polio, tetanus, diphtheria. Had she missed one she wondered. Her arm had felt like a pin cushion. Then to the chemists to obtain various malaria pills, mosquito repellent and antihistamine cream.

Her thoughts were interrupted by the sound of the front door opening and closing. The next minute her flatmate walked into the room and flopped down into the other armchair. Kathy was 5'7" tall, slim with long dark brown hair usually tied at the back in an elastic band. Susan was a little shorter at 5'6", medium build with brown shoulder length hair and a fringe.

'Hi Kath, busy day?'

'Yeh. We were running around like ferrets. The sunny day I suppose. How was your day?'

'Okay. I've been getting ready for tomorrow. I've just got to stuff it all in the backpack in the morning. When do you want to eat?'

'As soon as I have freshened up. I'm famished.'

'Good. I'll give Garcia's a ring and make sure they've got a table free.'

'Garcia's?'

'Yep. I thought we could live it up tonight and visit our favourite restaurant. It might be my last decent meal for months. It's a camping trip so probably be eating baked beans from now on.'

'Now I am glad I'm not going,' laughed Kathy. 'You and beans never were a good combination! Give me twenty minutes and I'll be ready.'

Forty minutes later they set off. The flat was less than a mile from the restaurant which was at the far end of the high street. On the way they passed the café that Kathy managed, dark and quiet now in the gloom.

As they entered the restaurant they were greeted by the owner.

'Good evening ladies. I have reserved you a table in your favourite position by the window.'

'Thanks Luigi' said Susan.

They walked over to the table and sat down. It was early in the evening and the restaurant was nearly empty, only one other couple, but it would soon start to get busy. They studied the menu. Both of them liked Italian and the food and service here were always good.

'I'm going to have the spaghetti carbonara with a side salad,' said Susan, 'how about you?'

'Definitely a pizza' replied Kathy. 'Not sure which one though. Maybe the four seasons.'

'How about drinks? Would you like to share a bottle of wine?'

'Sure. Chardonnay perhaps?'

'Sounds good to me.'

A waiter soon appeared and the order was taken. They didn't have long to wait before a bottle and two glasses arrived. The waiter uncorked the bottle and filled the glasses, then headed back towards the kitchen. They each took a mouthful.

'Ah, that's nice' purred Kathy. 'I needed that.'

'Same here.'

Kathy suddenly picked up her handbag and started rummaging in it.

'What are you looking for?' asked Susan.

'Nearly forgot this. Look what I found in the park earlier.' She rummaged some more and eventually produced a wooden object.

'What's that?'

'No idea. But thought you might have fun working it out. You like solving puzzles and this certainly is.' She handed it to her friend. 'What do you reckon Susie?'

Susan went quiet as she looked at it intently. The hexagonal piece was made of a fine grained light brown wood, less than three inches across in size. One side was plain except for a random sprinkling of silver stars. The other side had a gold hexagonal/circular motif around seven symbols. These were also in gold. One of the outer symbols looked like a capital P and another looked like an R. The central one reminded her of a design for the sun.

'It is strange' she said at last taking another sip of her wine. 'I've never seen such symbols before. Maybe some ancient script; and it is odd that each edge has a narrow groove in it. Almost looks as if this is only part of something. But what I wonder. It's pretty though whatever it is.'

'It beats me. Maybe it is some form of good luck charm?'

'Possibly but somehow I don't think so.'

'Who was for the pizza?'

Both girls jumped as they had not heard the waiter arrive.

'That's mine' said Kathy.

The waiter laid down the pizza and the spaghetti dish, and then scurried off, quickly returning with a salad.

'Thanks' said Susan, then turning towards Kathy 'This looks good.'

'Sure does. Great idea of yours.'

The two women tucked into their meals.

'More wine?' said Kathy after a while, picking up the bottle.

'Yes please,' then after a pause, 'I shall miss this when I am away.'

'What – the wine and the handsome waiter?' joked Kathy.

'No silly, us having a night out.'

'I know. So shall I.'

They carried on eating; both thoroughly enjoying the meal. When the main course was over they chatted for a bit.

'Wonder what sweets they have?' said Susan.

They looked at the dessert menu.

'Cheesecake and ice-cream for me.'

'Snap' replied Susan.

It wasn't long before the waiter came over, took the dessert order and removed the empty plates. They both had a sip of wine.

'Take this with you tomorrow' said Kathy, prodding the wooden hexagonal. 'You'll need something to think about during those long nights in the tent. Perhaps it will bring you luck.'

'Okay. Maybe someone on the trip will be a specialist on symbols.'

'Best hope he is good looking then.'

The two girls laughed. Susan popped the tablet into her bag. The dessert arrived. They each picked up a spoon and started eating.

'Scrumptious' said Susan.

Kathy was too busy eating to reply so just nodded. Eventually they both finished leaving two empty dishes. Susan topped up their glasses with the remainder of the wine.

'Here's to your tour of Africa,' said Kathy as she chinked the glasses together. The two girls took a sip of wine, looking out of the window as a few noisy youths passed by.

'Must visit the little room' said Kathy as she picked up her handbag. 'Are you having coffee?'

'Yes I think so.'

'Okay. I'll order it on my way back.'

She headed to the back of the restaurant. Susan lost herself in her thoughts. Presently she noticed her friend talking to Luigi.

Kathy returned and sat down.

'Coffee is on its way.'

Not long after the waiter came over with a tray and placed two cups of coffee on the table. He then placed a saucer containing some chocolate mints, some cheeses and some biscuits.

'We've not ordered cheese' said Susan in surprise.

'Special treat from the manager' said the waiter. 'He doesn't want you to go hungry while you are away.'

The waiter retired from the table.

'How did – what did you say to Luigi?'

'Just that you have a long journey to make in order to find a man.'

'You didn't?'

'Course not, only the first bit.'

'I don't know how your customers put up with you' said Susan smiling. They chatted light-heartedly, ate some cheese and sipped their coffees. Later Susan disappeared to the restroom. The bill was requested and they headed to the cash desk to pay.

'Thanks Luigi, a super meal as always.'

'My pleasure ladies. Coffee and cheese are on the house.' Turning to Susan, 'have a good trip. I shall look forward to hearing all about it when you return. Maybe you will meet a handsome young man.'

The girls said farewell and left the restaurant.

'You said you hadn't mentioned finding a man to Luigi' questioned Susan.

'I hadn't – honest' replied Kathy sincerely.

The next day both were up early. It was Saturday the 1st of November, the start of the tour. Susan wanted to finish packing and Kathy had to get to work.

'What time are your parents coming?' said Kathy as she headed to the front door.

'About one.'

'Okay, I'll be back by then. See you later.'

Susan heard the door open and close. All went quiet. She suddenly felt rather lonely. This won't do she thought to herself. She busied herself with the packing going through the list she had made out to make sure that nothing was forgotten. Once finished she changed the bed and tidied the room. By nine all was done. She had three clear hours before she had to be back to prepare lunch; plenty of time to call in at the library. She put on her coat, found a pencil and notepad which she placed in her bag then set off.

She had intended to take a short cut through the park but on reaching it found that the gate was closed. Unusual she thought as it was always open by now. Never mind she would go the slightly longer way round via the road.

On reaching the library, she entered and made her way to the information desk.

'Can I help you' said the assistant.

'Yes, do you have any books on ancient scripts and symbols?'

'Yes we do. Follow me and we will see what is on the shelf.' The assistant got up and Susan followed her over to one of the large book shelves.

'Now let me see – yes, here we are. There appear to be three books on ancient symbols and runes.'

'Thanks.' The assistant returned to the desk and Susan picked up one of the books – "The Magic of Runes". She opened it up and glanced at a few pages. She then scooped up the other two as well and took them over to a free table. She sat down, placed the books and her bag on top and reopened the first book. She flicked through a few pages till she came to one that featured pictures of a set of runes. She read the opening explanation. "The rune set illustrated below is based on the Northumbrian runes, a later version of the Anglo-Saxon runes. The symbol for Yr is the only real difference. A complete set has 30 runes, the last one being blank." She recognised two of the symbols. Maybe she had struck lucky at the first attempt. She took out the wooden tablet and compared the symbols. All of the outer ones looked similar to the picture although the one called ur was a little different. The middle symbol wasn't featured however. She sketched the six outer symbols in her notepad and then placed their names alongside; ur, thorn, rad, wyn, eoh, and lagu. She closed the first book, placed it to one side then selected another – "Runes and their Meanings". Again she opened it and flicked through a few pages till she found a picture of runes. "These runes are known as the Elder Futhark" the text said "the name taken from the first six letters, f, u, th, a, r, and k." She picked up the first book and compared the two sets of runes. There were a few differences notably rune number six and rune number twelve. This book gave the corresponding letter for each rune. The outer six on the tablet translated as u, th, r, w, æ and l. She made some more notes. The Elder Futhark runes corresponded exactly with the symbols on the tablet again with the exception of the centre one. She picked up the third book and glanced through. This book was more concerned with fortune telling so she set this one aside. She picked up the second book and read some more. "The runes come in sets of eight called ætts. The Elder Futhark has 24 runes in total." She made more notes and carried on reading. She had known nothing about runes until now. Apparently early runic symbols dated back to the Bronze Age and had been evolving ever since. There were a whole variety of runes, each differing slightly from their predecessors. Fascinating she thought. She carried on reading hoping to find some mention of the centre symbol but there was nothing. She put the book down at last and glanced at her watch. It was eleven thirty five. Good grief, how had the time got so late? She put the tablet, pencil and notepad in her bag and gathered up the books, replacing them on the shelf.

She left the library and made a detour to the butchers where she purchased some ham. She then walked directly home, noticing that the park was still closed. A good morning's work she mused as she reached the flat and let herself in.

She threw her coat onto one of the chairs, extracted the ham from her bag and went into the kitchen. Very soon she had made a salad and was boiling some potatoes. She heard the front door bell ring and went to answer it.

'Oh, hi Kath. Where's your key?'

'I can't find it. Must be here some place.'

Susan went back into the kitchen. Presently Kathy entered.

'All packed I see."

'Yes. Completed that first thing. I spent most of the morning in the library. I went to see what I could dig up about symbols.'

'And?'

'The librarian pointed me in the right direction. There were three books, two of which were quite useful. Those symbols are runes, at least the outer six are. Apparently there are lots of different types of runes, dependant on where and when they were developed. The runes on the tablet appear to be Elder Futhark.'

'Elder who?'

'Elder Futhark.'

'There's no need to swear.'

Susan turned to see her friend grinning.

'The Futhark bit is the first six letters, f, u, th, a, r and k; like alphabet is from alpha, beta.'

'So what did it say?'

'Well, that is the problem. The letters on the tablet translate as u, th, r, w, æ and l which doesn't seem to spell anything.' Susan turned off the gas and strained the potatoes. 'And I could find no mention of the central character.'

'Maybe the letters stand for something.'

'I never thought of that. But if they do I've no idea what.' Susan put the potatoes into a dish and sprinkled on some herbs then placed a knob of butter on the top. Meanwhile Kathy took some plates from the cupboard and laid the table. The front door bell rang. Susan went to the door and opened it. It was her parents Ron and Joan Scarlet. She ushered them inside.

'Good timing' said Susan, 'I've just finished preparing lunch. Here, let me take your coats.' Kathy walked into the lounge and after the usual hellos the four of them walked into the kitchen.

'Where shall we sit?' said Joan.

'You sit here mum, and dad here then I can get to the oven.' Joan, Ron and Kathy sat down while Susan served the ham and placed the still warm potatoes and salad on the table. Susan then sat down as well.

'Nice to be waited on' said Kathy. They tucked into lunch. This was followed by apple crumble and custard.

'Anyone for tea?' asked Kathy.

'That would be great' answered Ron. Kathy got up, filled the kettle and set it on the gas. Then she cleared the table, attended to the cups and saucers, and filled a milk jug. She sat down again.

'Are you all prepared' asked Joan looking at her daughter. 'Have you packed your toothbrush and soap and towel?'

'Yes mum. I've got everything I shall need. If I pack any more I shan't be able to pick up the rucksack.'

'You are going for five months you know.'

'It's okay. There will be places to buy things if I run out of anything.'

'What time is your train?' asked Ron.

'3.28.'

'If we leave here at a quarter to three that should give us plenty of time to drive to the station and buy your ticket. It's just after two at the moment.'

'That sounds good.'

The kettle boiled and Kathy made the tea. They nattered over their drinks until it was time to depart.

'It's time to go. Have you got your passport and money?'
'Yes dad.'
'Okay. I'll take your rucksack to the car.' Susan took her other bag and went with her dad. Her mum followed. Kathy took the spare key from the drawer, closed the front door after her and joined them. Joan sat in the front seat and the girls in the back.

They set off for the station. Only two streets away Kathy prodded Susan and pointed out of the window.

'See that guy there,' Susan turned her head to see a tall, thin man in an overcoat, 'he was in the café this morning. He only ordered a coffee but sat around for ages. I caught him coming out of the office and he made the excuse he had been looking for the toilet but I don't believe that at all. I've never seen him in before and there was something about him that I didn't like. Anyhow nothing seemed to have been taken so hopefully he was just some weirdo and he won't be in again.'

The traffic was light and they made good time, reaching the station about three. Ron parked the car. They all got out, Ron taking Susan's rucksack from the boot. They then proceeded to the booking office. Susan lined up, there were only a couple of people in front of her, and had soon purchased her ticket.

'Your train will be coming in on platform three' said Kathy.

'I'll try and phone you all from Gibraltar in about a week's time' said Susan 'otherwise it will be a postcard.'

'I will write to you at the poste restante' said Joan.

'You'll like Gibraltar' said Ron 'I was there at the end of the war.'

'Bye mum, dad' as she gave each a kiss and got several in exchange. 'Bye Kath. Be good.' She gave her friend a big hug. 'I shall miss you.'

'Take care Susie. I shall miss you too.'

Susan struggled to put on the rucksack. She then walked forward, showing her ticket to the collector on the way. Before she went down the slope to the platform she turned and waved. A tear came to her eye and she brushed it aside.

The train arrived on time and she got on board. Luckily it wasn't very busy so she sat by the window and put her luggage beside her. A whistle sounded and they were off. It was the start of her big adventure.

Chapter Two

'Yesterday didn't go according to plan' sighed the tall, thin man standing gazing out of the window at the surrounding tower blocks and small tenement buildings that were typical of this area of London. It was late afternoon and the sun had slipped below the horizon. 'The target, a short elderly man, had the tablet in his pocket. I followed him and as he took a short cut through the park I decided to take the opportunity and relieve him of it. There was no-one in sight so I came up behind him and caused him to stumble and fall. As I made to help him to his feet I took the tablet from his coat.' He had turned round now and was facing the man to whom he was speaking. This man was seated at a desk upon which lay an opened newspaper.

'So what went wrong?' asked Bill.

'The bloke must have noticed or suspected something for he checked his pockets, noticed its absence, and lunged at me. I grabbed him by the throat and dragged him behind some thick evergreens where I was able to subdue him. Unfortunately I then lost my bearings and came out from the bushes in a totally different area of the park. By the time I realised my mistake and retraced my steps the tablet was nowhere to be seen. Looking around in a panic I noticed a girl heading towards one of the entrances. There was nobody else about so I guessed that she must have picked it up. I followed her. She walked to a nearby café, the Rainbow Rooms, and entered. I watched from afar and soon realised that she had not gone in for a drink but worked there. I had hoped to follow her home but it was dark when she left and I lost her on the busy high street.'

'Does that mean you have lost it, Matt?'

'Well yes and no. This morning I went into the café as a customer. I discovered her name is Kathy Rand and in a busy moment was able to get into the office and check her bag.'

'And?'

'Nothing. I then reasoned that she must have taken it out of her bag the previous evening. So I found out where she lives, she shares a flat with a friend, and this afternoon I was able to search it.'

'So you have it?'

'No. It wasn't there. But I did find some notes on runes that somebody had made and I am confident that the tablet is now with her friend, a girl called Susan Scarlet. I shall get it back from her tomorrow, don't worry.'

There was silence for a while. Bill rose, took hold of his empty cup and walked over to the sink. Matt took a small tobacco tin from his pocket and rolled himself a cigarette. He lit it with a match and inhaled deeply, blowing out a long thin stream of smoke that hung in the air. He was dressed in a dark suit which fitted loosely on his thin frame. His white shirt looked slightly dingy but the neatly knotted tie helped to smarten his overall appearance. Bill was of medium height and build. He was wearing a roll-necked sweater, coloured gold except for a ring of light and dark brown diamonds around the base. This overlapped a pair of corduroy trousers. He was in his late fifties, about twenty years older than Matt. They were in a self-contained flat on the top floor of a three storey building. The large room was divided into three areas; kitchen, living room and bedroom. A door at the bedroom end led to a rather cramped bathroom. The floor was carpeted except for the kitchen area which was covered in linoleum tiles. The room was sparsely furnished, only containing a bed, a wardrobe, a desk and two wooden chairs which once had formed a set of four.

Bill returned to his desk with two cups of tea. Matt reached over and took one, at the same time stubbing out his cigarette in the ashtray on the desk. Bill opened the drawer of the desk and took out a packet of chocolate digestive biscuits. He offered them to Matt, who declined, then extracted one for himself and proceeded to munch it merrily. It was Matt who broke the silence.

'How many pieces do we have now?'

Bill replied through a mouthful of half chewed biscuit.

'Eh?' grunted Matt, who didn't understand the response to his question.

'Four' repeated Bill, who had hastily swallowed the biscuit. 'We have also located another. It has been traced to a private collection of unusual artefacts. Its owner will be persuaded to part with it.'

'What's so special about these wooden objects?'

'Let's just say they are unique and that is what gives them their value.'

Matt was pensive for a bit. He was tired of trailing people and was thinking he would go out tonight for a few beers. He drained his cup, rose and put on his overcoat.

'I must be on my way.'

Matt departed. Bill rearranged the paper so that the crossword was in a convenient position. He then helped himself to another biscuit and proceeded to tackle the first clue. As usual he had forgotten his tea but then he liked it cold anyway.

'Thanks for dropping me back at work Ron' said Kathy.

'No problem at all.'

'Bye' said Joan.

Kathy closed the door and the car pulled away. A few steps along the road she entered the café.

'Hi Paul. How's it going?'

'Yeh, okay. It's been steady but nothing I couldn't handle.'

'I knew you would cope, thanks. When you have completed what you're doing shoot off home. I'll finish off.'

'Righto.'

Paul beavered away cleaning the last few tables, grabbed his coat and headed out of the door. Kathy went into the office and sorted out a few orders for the following week. She then washed the last few dirty items of crockery and checked that all was ready for Monday. It was five o'clock. Not bad she thought to herself. She put on her coat, grabbed her bag and left, double locking the door on her exit. Within fifteen minutes she was home.

She turned the key and entered the flat. It was eerily quiet. She turned on the light and closed the front door. I am going to have to get used to this she thought, coming home to an empty house. She took off her coat and hung it up. She then walked through the lounge into the kitchen, poured herself a glass of fruit juice from the fridge and returned to the lounge. Putting the glass on a side table she kicked off her shoes and sat down pulling her legs up beside her. Ah, that's better she thought. She picked up the juice and aimlessly gazed across the room. She had a feeling that something had changed in the room; probably Susan had moved something before she had left, but on thinking back realised she had been the last to leave. What was it? She slowly looked from left to right. Her eyes settled on the sideboard. She put down the glass and walked over to it. The only additional item on the top were some notes on runes that Susan had left her; otherwise just the usual things, a carriage clock, a couple of framed pictures, some keys, some loose change and an elastic band. She sat down again, tucked her legs up and drank her fruit juice. She needed to unwind. She got up and put on one of her favourite cassettes, Simon and Garfunkel. That's more relaxing she thought as she settled down again.

An hour or so later Kathy was in the kitchen making herself a snack. Her mind wandered and eventually came to rest thinking of Susan and whether she had met up with her group okay. She could just picture her staggering along under the weight of her rucksack. She would be – 'that's what's wrong' she suddenly said out loud; 'the picture is not there.' Walking briskly into the lounge she walked over to the sideboard. Yes, it was gone. The photo had been wedged in front of one of the framed pictures. She checked to see if it had fallen down but there was no sign of it. It was a photograph of the two of them at Susan's thirty first birthday party. Joan had taken it and had only dropped it round a few days before. Now it was missing. It was a good picture of them both having fun and the only recent one they had of themselves together. She was sure that Susan wouldn't have taken it with her, so who had and why? She shuddered. Someone must have been in the flat. She quickly checked the two bedrooms and the bathroom. On the face of it nothing seemed amiss. She then did a more detailed search of her bedroom, examining each cupboard drawer in turn. The items in one drawer had moved, or was her imagination playing tricks. She then searched Susan's room but couldn't see that anything was wrong. Am I making this all up she asked herself? No I am not she thought angrily. That photo was definitely there earlier. Who the hell has been snooping around our flat she wondered. And how did they get in?

She went to the front door and bolted it. Once in the

lounge she turned on the electric heater. It had got cold. Returning to the kitchen she resumed where she had left off and finished fixing her snack. This she ate at the table, washing it down with a glass of water. Back in the lounge she snuggled down in the armchair and tried to reason things through. She wished Susan was there to talk it over with. Whoever had broken in must have done so after they had gone to the station. So what had the person been looking for? Nothing of importance had been taken, only a personal photograph. Then she thought of the customer she had found coming out of the office. Was there a connection. Had he been searching for something? I don't own anything of value that I know of and the takings from the café are placed in the bank regularly. Surely it can't concern that wooden tablet I found. Well if it is they are out of luck, she thought, for its heading to Africa.

The train was on time when it arrived at Portsmouth and Southsea. Susan alighted and plonked her luggage on the platform. She was familiar with the station as she had visited Portsmouth several times before. The meeting time was not until six so she had over forty minutes to spare. She put on her rucksack and descended the stairs to the booking hall and meeting place. I expect I shall be the first to arrive she thought. She passed through the ticket barrier and into the hall. It was empty. She found a bench and sat down, placing her luggage beside her. She felt nervous and hoped she would like the others on the trip. As she gazed around the station she noticed a girl appear with a large pack. This person, on seeing her, strolled over. She was in her twenties, tall, with short auburn hair.

'Hi! Are you on the Africa Slowly tour?'
'Yes' said Susan feeling strangely lost for words.

'Likewise. My name's Rosemary.' She put out her hand.

'And I'm Susan' she said, shaking it. Then after a pause, 'have you done anything like this before?'

'Yes. A couple of years ago I travelled to India. I loved it, so saved up to do this one. It should be fun. Looks like we have another for the tour' she said, pointing across the concourse. Sure enough another girl also in her twenties was walking in their direction. She had long blond hair.

'Hello. Are you travelling with Trans-Africa?' she asked.

'Yes' said the two girls.

'Oh good. I am Ellie from Finland.' Susan and Rosemary introduced themselves. Rosemary noticed some activity near the entrance, and brought the others attention to it.

'I'll check it out' she said, picking up her pack. She walked across to the door, turned and beckoned them to join her. This they did. Outside a number of people were milling about, some men and some women. Susan thought most were in their late twenties or thirties but noticeably a couple were much older.

Presently they were shepherded into taxis for the drive to the international ferry terminal. She shared the cab with Rosemary and Ellie. At the port they met the second driver, Neil and the cook, Alison, both from England. They were instructed to put their main luggage on the truck but keep anything they needed for the crossing in their day bag which they should keep with them. Susan looked up at the truck. It seemed massive. The tailgate, which had been lowered, transformed into two steps. When it was her turn she climbed up the steps with her luggage. Once inside, the vehicle seemed much more cramped. The opposite to Dr Who's Tardis she mused. There were two long rows of cushioned seats facing inwards, each comprised of five lockable sections. Under the front four sections on each side, the space underneath had been split into three compartments. Each person had one compartment only in which to store their belongings. She chose one nearer to the front of the vehicle. There was an overhead rack for her sleeping bag. It was good to be rid of her backpack she thought. She exited down the steps and made her way to the departure lounge.

Once everyone had packed away their things the tour leader, Colin, also from England, introduced himself. There were eighteen on the tour, two short of the maximum of twenty that the truck could accommodate. He went through the itinerary for the next few days. They were going to take the ferry to Le Havre, then drive south through France and onward to the south of Spain. He then handed each person a key tied on a shoelace. This key would open every padlock on the truck enabling them to get to their lockers and any equipment they might need. The key was best worn round the neck so as to keep it safe. Lastly he explained about the buzzer. This was located in the passenger section of the vehicle and was to be used for passing messages to the driver in the cab. The codes were to be as follows: when the truck was stationary – one buzz if someone was getting on or off and two buzzes if they were ready to go; when the truck was moving – one buzz for an emergency stop, two buzzes for a photo stop and three buzzes for a toilet stop. He then departed.

They were eventually allowed to board; the ship finally getting underway at eleven. Susan found herself sitting with five others of the group. There were Rosemary and Ellie whom she had met earlier together with Geoff from New Zealand, Rebecca from Norwich, and Richard from Hastings. The conversation was light-hearted and mostly centred around the tour. Only Rosemary had any major travel experience, the rest had jumped in at the deep end like she had. Susan felt relaxed for the first time since leaving home.

Chapter Three

Matt looked at his watch. It was just before eleven on Sunday morning. He was sitting in his car which was parked a little way from the flat yet still offering a good view. Nobody had entered or left it since he had arrived. He had a bit of a hangover from last night. I could do with a coffee he thought; I hope this isn't going to be a wasted day.

Now where did I put my bag Kathy wondered; ah here it is. Her parents had invited her for Sunday lunch. They had hinted that she might be at a loose end with Susan being away and they had been right. She was looking forward to it. Her brother would also be there and she hadn't seen him for ages. She checked the time. Yes, if I leave now I will catch the next bus. She put on her coat and departed.

Matt's eyes were feeling heavy. He closed them then opened them again. Must keep alert he thought. He reached into his pocket and pulled out a packet of gums. He popped one into his mouth and started to suck it. Just then he noticed someone had emerged from the house. It was Kathy Rand. She was alone. She started to walk down the road in the direction of the high street. He watched for a bit then got out of the car and followed her from a discreet distance. She turned left and eventually he did the same, but rather than follow he waited to see which way she was heading. He soon found out as she halted at the bus stop. Excellent he thought. He retraced his steps back to the flat. He pulled a photo from his pocket, glanced at it, then returned it. He rang the front door bell and waited. There was no answer. He rang again but still no response. Where was she he wondered? Taking the key from his pocket he let himself in. Nothing stirred. He checked the rooms but nobody was there. Odd he thought. He had another quick look for the tablet but drew a blank as he had expected. He cast his mind back to yesterday when he had watched them leave in the car. He remembered seeing a man carrying out a large bag and putting it in the boot. Then he recalled seeing a travel brochure in one of the bedrooms. He went into Susan's room. It was exactly as he had left it on his last visit. The bed had not been slept in. He spotted the travel brochure and flicked through it. A tour had been highlighted. Its date of departure was yesterday. So where have you gone Miss Scarlet, he asked himself. The brochure answered Nairobi. His heart sank. Of all the luck he cursed. He rolled up the brochure and put it in his inside pocket, then checking that the coast was clear, left the flat and walked to the car. The engine started first time and he drove away.

The truck pulled up at the campsite early in the afternoon. They had driven down from Le Havre. During the journey Susan had got to know, or at least found out the names of, the other passengers. If her memory was correct they were Chris, Louisa and Steve from Australia, Johanne and Kevin from Canada, Ellie from Finland, Udo from Germany, Henriette and Kees from the Netherlands, Geoff from New Zealand, Carol from the United States, Andrew, Anita, Barbara, Rebecca, Richard, Rosemary and herself from the United Kingdom. All were travelling alone except Andrew and Anita.

They were all seated now on camping stools. Colin was explaining about the daily routines. Whenever they camped or stopped for lunch two bowls of water and a bar of soap were to be placed on the ground near to the rear of the truck. These were to be used to wash ones hands after a visit to the toilet or before handling food. When preparing food the fruit and vegetables would be soaked in water containing a couple of crystals of potassium permanganate for ten minutes to kill any bacteria. When the jerry cans, there were twenty one of them, were refilled with water they were to be purified before use. He then went on to talk about the duty rosters. These were necessary for the smooth running of the tour. There would be three duties: 1 – getting out the tents, sleeping mats, large table, stools and cooking equipment; 2 – putting away the said items; 3 – cooking and washing up. Each group would spend two days in turn at each duty followed by six days of rest. Susan joined Louisa and Richard in group C. In the meantime Alison and Neil had got the tents and sleeping mats out of the truck. These were all numbered and whichever ones they chose they would keep for the duration of the tour.

'Would you like to share a tent?' asked Rebecca. Rebecca was 27, 5'3" tall with dark brown hair cut in a bob.

'Sure' replied Susan.

They picked up tent four and mats three and twenty two.

'Shall we set it up over there?'

'Okay, that looks a good spot' agreed Rebecca.

They carried it over and took it out of its bag. There was an instruction leaflet which they glanced at. It started to rain.

'Just what we need' said Susan, 'let's wait a bit till it eases.'

This they did. It was only a quick shower and soon over. They unrolled the tent and pinned down the base with the pegs provided. They then put together the poles. Two of these had to be used to raise the tent by inserting the protruding spikes into the holes at the top of the tent.

'I'll do that' said Rebecca.

She dived into the fabric of the tent. Susan watched as the tent moved this way then that and finally collapsed altogether. Hysterical laughter could be heard coming from within. Susan peered inside to find Rebecca in a fit of giggles. She laughed also.

'Sorry' she said finally 'I'll try that again.'

This time the tent became upright and Susan slotted on the connecting pole. Rebecca emerged.

'Wonder where these plastic tubes go?' asked Susan, looking for the instructions.

'Here they are' replied Rebecca picking up a sodden piece of paper which had been blown into a puddle by a gust of wind.

'They must go on the top of the spikes I guess.'

She put them on top and the two of them draped over the flysheet, pinning it into position. The guy rope was also pegged down and made taut.

'Not bad' commented Andrew who was passing.

'Thanks' said Rebecca.

On his arrival Bill was making a drink. Matt wondered if he ever left the building as he was always in whenever he called. Bill found a second cup and presently brought over two cups of tea.

'Good news or bad?'

'Both' explained Matt who was trying to be optimistic. He told Bill of his earlier visit to the girl's flat and his realisation that the tablet had just embarked on a journey.

'So what is the good news?'

'I have purchased a ticket on tomorrows crossing to Le Havre. Although I shall be two days behind them I can catch that up as I drive south. They are due to visit the Alhambra in Granada on their way down to Gibraltar. The truck they are travelling in is slow and will stick out like a sore thumb. I should be able to get the tablet at one place or the other.'

'The sooner the better or you might find that you are out of a job. I won't finance your mistakes indefinitely do you hear? You do know what this girl looks like I hope.'

'Of course' Matt replied confidently, feeling in his pocket for the photo.

'What time do you leave?'

'About five in the afternoon.'

Bill was now munching on a custard cream. Matt drank his tea.

Chapter Four

It was nine in the morning and Matt hadn't been up long when the phone rang. He answered it on the sixth ring.

'Hello – yes – hi Bill – yes, I've got time – okay, see you later.' He put the phone down. I wonder what's up he thought; Bill seems anxious to see me.

Kathy was serving in the café. It was always busy at this hour with breakfasts. The door opened and in walked Barry, a lorry driver and regular customer. He walked up to the counter.

'Hi Kathy, the usual please.'

'No problem it's on its way.'

Barry sat down while Kathy cracked a couple of eggs in the pan and added some rashers of bacon. They began to sizzle. She then set about making him a mug of black coffee.

'Have you seen todays paper?' asked Barry.

'No, why?'

'Apparently there has been a murder in the nearby park.'

'You're joking. What's it say?'

Barry read the opening paragraph.

'A man was found dead early on Saturday morning by a lady out walking her dog. He had died of asphyxiation. The man was in his seventies, 5'2" tall, bald and had been wearing a long dark grey raincoat. The police are treating his death as murder and are appealing for witnesses who may have seen him, his attacker or anyone acting suspiciously in the area, to contact them.'

Kathy came over with the coffee, placed it on the table and looked at the paper. It read "Mystery of Dead Man in Bush". She went back to the kitchen, finished cooking the breakfast and brought it over.

'When do they think he was killed?'

'It says here sometime Friday morning.'

'Friday? I walked through the park on Friday. I was coming back from the post office and as it was a nice day made a small detour.'

'Did you see anything odd?' asked Barry.

'No, nothing.'

Another customer had come in and Kathy went around the counter to serve.

It was early that afternoon when Matt arrived. Bill ushered him in.

'Good, glad you could make it. Take a seat. Have you seen today's newspaper?'

'No.'

'There have been developments. Here, take a look while I make some drinks.'

Bill passed Matt the newspaper. The headline read "Man Murdered in Park." Matt read the article through. As he finished Bill came over with two cups of tea.

'It looks as though you are in the clear for the time being. There is no mention of the tablet and the police have no leads.'

'I thought he was still alive when I left him. Still, if he had had any sense he would have accepted our offer.'

'Ah, that brings me nicely to the other developments. Karl was able to get the fifth tablet. The guy who owned it was happy to part with it for a reasonable price.' Matt had been rolling a cigarette and was lighting it at that moment so nodded. 'Your Miss Scarlet has the sixth tablet which just leaves the seventh. Its last known whereabouts were in Morocco and as you are heading that way I want you to track it down.'

'Do we know which town?'

'No.' Bill had extracted a packet of bourbon biscuits from the drawer of his desk and after offering them to Matt had taken one himself. He started eating it.

'Guess I've got my work cut out finding the seventh one.'

They sat in silence for a bit. Matt smoked his cigarette and drank his tea. Bill had another biscuit.

'I'll need a guide book for Morocco.'

'It just so happens that I have one here.' Bill opened the drawer of the desk and took out an up to date copy of a popular guidebook. 'Take this, and keep me informed regularly.'

Susan was sitting in the truck, together with Rebecca, Richard and Kevin. Richard was 30, 5'7", slim with brown wavy hair and glasses. Kevin was 32, 5'9", thickset with fair hair. It was a fine evening and the others were sitting outside. Tents had been erected and the evening meal had been cleared away. She had started a journal and was searching her bag for a pen when she came upon the tablet.

'Oh I had forgotten about this' she said, addressing nobody in particular.

'What's that?' asked Rebecca.

'This' replied Susan passing the tablet to her. 'My friend gave it to me the day before we left England.'

'O, that's nice. What do all the symbols mean?'

'Well the letters are runes.' Susan found her notepad and opened it. 'According to the book in the library the letters translate as u, th, r, w, æ and l.'

Richard and Kevin had stopped what they were doing and were looking across at the girls.

'May I have a look?' asked Richard.

'Of course' replied Susan.

Rebecca passed him the tablet. Richard studied it then passed it on to Kevin. Once Kevin had finished with it Richard had another look.

'These stars on the back,' he said 'they look a bit like a constellation. I can't make anything of the symbols. 'Where did your friend get it?' He passed it back to Susan.

'Kathy, my flatmate, found it in the local park.'

'I wonder if it is part of something else' commented Richard.

'Funny you should say that because I thought exactly the same.'

Susan put it away and wrote up her diary.

Chapter Five

Kathy was at home watching the evening news on the television. There was not that much of interest on it and she was contemplating switching channels when the newscaster read 'The police have discovered the identity of the dead man found in a park in south London. He is Franz Miller from Dusseldorf in West Germany.' Kathy listened intently. 'He was a leading specialist in scientific art and had been working with colleagues in the British Museum. On the day of his death it is believed that he had gone to meet a prospective buyer of a piece of art that he had recently been researching. It is unknown whether the meeting took place however the item in question has gone missing and the police are keen to meet with this buyer so that they can eliminate him from their enquiries.' The newscaster continued onto another topic but Kathy had stopped listening. Wow, she thought, I wonder if that tablet I found is the missing piece of art.

Several miles away Bill had also heard the news. He was not happy.

Chapter Six

Having visited Poitiers, Bordeaux and San Sebastian, the tour had arrived at a campsite to the north of Granada. The C group had been on cooking duties and now the meal was over they were washing up the pans. Susan was reflecting on how life on the truck had developed a certain routine; get up, wash, eat breakfast, brush teeth, refill water bottle, take down tent, attend to camp duties, join scramble to get to ones locker; leave camp, either watch scenery or read or play cards, dice or scrabble, stopping to eat lunch and buy food; arrive at camp, attend to camp duties, put up tent, wash, eat dinner, take malaria pills, free time, go to bed. Her life was far removed from her job in the bank. Each day there were new sights to see and experiences to be had and she was enjoying every minute; well maybe not every minute as she didn't particularly like washing-up. She smiled to herself.

'What are you thinking about?' asked Richard who had been watching her. 'You can't be enjoying scrubbing that pan surely.'

'Hm. Oh, I was miles away. I was thinking about this trip and how much I was enjoying it, but not the washing-up.'

'I agree with you there. Still, only tomorrow to go then we are off duties for a while. Neil and Alison mentioned about going to a nearby bar in a bit, and it is Friday night. Do you fancy joining them?'

'Yes, I could just do with a drink; this is thirsty work.'

'Good. Bring that tablet and your notes with you. Let's see if we can decipher it. I like solving puzzles.'

'Yes, me too.'

Susan scrubbed with renewed vigour.

'Are you coming Louisa?' enquired Richard.

'Sure thing.'

Seven of them headed off to the bar. It was a small rustic place with solid wooden furniture. Tonight it was quite busy with what appeared to be the local populace. Drinks were purchased and they found somewhere to sit. Louisa and Kevin joined Neil and Alison on one table while Susan, Rebecca and Richard sat at another.

'Here's to our tour of Africa' said Richard, raising his glass. The other two did likewise.

'Cheers.' They each took a mouthful.

'Nice beer' commented Rebecca.

'Yes it is' agreed Susan. 'I usually drink wine but this is very refreshing.'

They drank their beers and chatted. Soon their glasses were empty.

'Who's for another?' asked Susan.

'Yes please.'

'I'll get them' said Richard standing up. He headed to the bar and returned with three bottles.

'Thanks.'

Susan reached into her bag and pulled out the tablet and her notepad.

'Okay' she said. 'Now let us see if we can work out what these symbols mean.' They each studied it in turn.

'What are the letter equivalents again?' asked Rebecca.

'U, th, r, w, ae, and l.'

'I can't think of many words beginning with ae except aegis, aeon, aerial, aeroplane, oh and aerate,' said Richard 'and having ae in the middle I can only think of Israel.'

'Well we can form the end of Israel as we have r, ae and l, however that would leave u, th and w which is not very promising' replied Susan.

'White aeroplane lands under the roof' uttered Rebecca suddenly.

'What?' they both said in unison.

'I was wondering if the initial letters maybe make a phrase.'

'That's what Kathy thought' said Susan, adding 'my flatmate back home.'

'Maybe the letters stand for numbers' suggested Richard 'which would give us' – he worked them out – '21, 20, 18, 23, 1, 12.'

'Oh sorry' said Susan apologetically 'I don't believe I told you but the runes are part of the Elder Futhark and the letters occur in a totally different order. The name Futhark is formed from the first six letters so u is the 2nd letter, th the 3rd and r the 5th. I cannot remember the other ones off hand.' She flicked through her notepad. 'Here we are, the w is the 8th, ae the 13th and l' – she counted them off – 'the 21st.' Richard was busy writing down the values.

'2, 3, 5, 8, 13, 21' he read. 'That seems familiar.'

'That's it' spluttered Susan rather loudly, attracting the attention of the surrounding tables who gazed in their direction. 'It's the Fibonacci series' continued Susan, much quieter now. 'The first two 1s are missing but otherwise it's the start of the series.'

'Of course.'

'Sorry but I don't get it' said Rebecca mystified.

'If you write down the first two numbers of the sequence 1, 1 and then add them you produce the third term, 2. Each term thereafter is the sum of the two preceding terms so 1+2=3, 2+3=5, 3+5=8, 5+8=13 and so on' explained Richard.

'Oh, I see.'

'It's a very important series for it occurs often in nature and it gives the irrational number phi, one term divided by its previous term for example 13 divided by 8' added Susan excitedly. Neil had walked over.

'We are heading back to camp soon so if you want to join us you had best finish your drinks.'

'Okay, thanks Neil.'

He returned to the others. Ten minutes later they headed back.

The hotel was very basic but Matt didn't care. He had made it to Granada ahead of the truck and that's all that mattered. He had eaten a good meal and was presently washing it down with a cold beer. Later he would relax with a cigarette. It was warmer than London and that had to be good. If only he could get the tablet from the girl tomorrow. Still, that was another day and he cast the thought from his mind. Right now he was enjoying this one.

Chapter Seven

Matt was up in good time and drove along to the Alhambra. He parked a short distance from it then walked up toward the entrance.

The truck arrived early in the morning. Colin was to stay with the vehicle for reasons of security. The rest of them followed Neil and Alison up to the Gate of Justice, the main entrance, and through to the ticket office. Neil purchased the tickets and once inside they were left to their own devices. Susan headed to the Royal Palace first, as did many of the group. This was all new to her. The 14th century palace had been built by the Moors. At school the history lessons had never touched on Spain so she was keen to learn more.

Their arrival had been noted. Matt had waited for them to enter then had entered also. He had bought a small guidebook which featured the layout of the place. If successful in his quest he wanted to know the position of the exit for a quick getaway. He kept one eye on Susan and one on the guidebook. She was surrounded by group members but as they progressed through the buildings he knew the group would split up. He had to be patient and to wait his chance. He just hoped that she was carrying the tablet and had not left it in the truck.

Susan walked through the Mexuar and came out onto the western side of the Myrtle Patio. The patio contained a long narrow pool surrounded by low hedges of myrtle, hence the name. Lovely she thought. She turned to her left and eventually found herself in the Ambassadors' Hall. The latticed cedar wood dome was inlaid with stars. She was amazed by the beauty of the design. She took a picture. Eventually she headed back to the Myrtle Patio, walking on the eastern side of it, and left into the Lions' Patio. The centrepiece of this area was a fountain seemingly supported on the back of twelve lions. It was superb. She tried to visualise how it might have been in years gone by but without much success. She took another photo. The next room on the right was the Hall of the Abencerrages. The room had an impressive dome ceiling. She noticed that Udo and Ellie stood nearby admiring it also.

Matt had Susan in his sights. As he had expected the group was slowly dispersing. Only six people were close to her now. I must be patient he told himself.

Having taken in the room Susan moved off towards the right and the Kings' Hall. Udo, Ellie and Louisa also headed that way. Not long after they continued into the next room leaving Susan by herself. This could be my chance thought Matt. He began to approach her. As he neared his target two blokes seemed to appear out of nowhere. He stopped abruptly.

'Hi Susan' a voice said.

Susan turned to see another visitor reading a guidebook and then Richard and Kevin heading towards her.

'Fabulous place isn't it?'

'Sure is' said Kevin. 'Have you seen the harem?'

'Yes, superb' answered Susan. 'I was just going to head to the Hall of Two Sisters and eventually to the gardens. Have you been there yet?'

'Not yet' said Richard.

'You're welcome to join me.'

'Okay.'

They headed off. Damn, thought Matt. So near. Never mind, there's still time. He followed at a distance.

As they approached the Generalife gardens they came upon Rebecca. Susan and Rebecca got into a conversation. They carried on walking, with Richard and Kevin a little ahead of the other two. The garden was bathed in sunlight. The two girls stopped by a seat. Susan sat down and rummaged in her bag producing a sunhat. She put it on. It's now or never thought Matt. He dashed from the cover of a hedge, grabbed the bag and ran.

'Hey' shouted Susan 'come back with that'.

She stood up to give chase. Rebecca who had been facing the other way spun round to see what was happening. Richard and Kevin, having heard the shout had turned and were starting to run. Susan hadn't fastened the bag and as Matt made off with it he noticed the contents were spilling out. He got a better grip on it but too late, the tablet had dropped to the ground. Rats he thought, if I stop and go back for it I will be caught, so he threw the bag and dodged behind another hedge and out of sight. Susan was first to the bag, followed closely by the others. They gathered up the contents and Susan checked to see if anything had been taken.

'It's all here I think, thanks.'

'Gee, I never thought that might happen here' said Rebecca.

'An opportunist thief I guess' commented Richard, 'you're lucky you didn't lose anything.'

'If I had gotten my hands on him I would have given him what for' said Kevin.

They retraced their steps.

'Let's check out the fountains' suggested Rebecca.

When it was time to leave they met with Neil and

recounted the earlier events. Sometimes get that in Africa but its most unusual here he had answered. I'll let Colin know.

They drove south through the Sierra Nevada Mountains then west along the coast road to Malaga, their stopping place for the night.

Matt was cursing his luck. He was driving the car back to the hotel to collect his belongings. So close to success; at least I know for certain that she has the tablet, he thought to himself, but now it is going to be nigh on impossible to get it.

Chapter Eight

She was walking down a path with hedges on either side of her. She wanted to get to the open area with lawns and fountains but somehow couldn't find it. There was no-one around to ask directions from. She wondered where Kathy was. I must hurry up she thought and get through these hedges, but her legs felt so heavy. She heard movement behind her. Someone was following. He was getting closer. Run she told herself but to no avail. Whoever it was had nearly caught her up. She had to see who it was. As she turned a tall thin man reached for her bag. She screamed.

'Susan, what's the matter?' asked Rebecca, sitting up in the tent.

'Where - ,' Susan looked panic-stricken.

'You're in the tent' said Rebecca calmly. 'You were dreaming. You're okay.'

She reached over to comfort her. Susan had come to now. Relief flooded across her face.

'Oh Becky. I was having a dreadful dream.' Susan recounted what she could recall of it. 'And when I turned to face him it was the same man I had seen on the way to the station.'

'Same as whom?' asked Rebecca, a bit bewildered.

'Sorry' said Susan. 'The man in my dream was the same guy as tried to pinch my bag in Granada; the same tall thin man Kathy had pointed out to me as we had driven to the railway station for the train to Portsmouth.' She told

Rebecca what Kathy had told her, of him visiting the café and being seen coming out of the office. 'I thought the man in the Alhambra looked somewhat familiar but dismissed it as imagination. Now I am sure it's the same man. He must have followed us here, which can only mean one thing; that he is after the tablet.'

'If that's true then that tablet must be more important than we had thought. Best keep it locked away on the truck from now on. In fact use my locker rather than yours.'

'Good idea Becky.'

They settled back down to sleep. There were still three more hours before morning.

They were staying at a campsite in San Roque. It was a large site in an area of trees. It contained the usual toilet and shower facilities plus a bar and restaurant. It was dawn and Rebecca was already up and doing. Susan dressed, went to the truck to get her wash bag and then walked across to the shower block. They were returning to the campsite that evening so there wasn't the usual rush to take the tent down. She felt a bit tired and lacked her usual ebullience. She lingered under the shower, finally returning as breakfast was being served. Dumping her wash bag in the tent she collected a bowl of porridge and sat down next to Rebecca and Richard. They had been talking but now were quiet. Richard smiled at her and she attempted to smile back.

'Sorry. I feel a bit flat this morning' she said.

'No problem. You'll be fine by the time we get to Gibraltar.'

He got up, walked over to the table and returned with some French toast; or eggy bread as the Aussies called it. It was one of Susan's favourites as it could be eaten as a savoury or sweet depending on how ones taste buds felt. Presently she went across with Rebecca and came back with a couple of slices. Once she had eaten she felt a little cheerier.

They left camp at half past eight and drove to Algeciras. Colin booked tickets for tomorrows ferry to Ceuta. They then doubled back and drove down to Gibraltar. It promised to be a nice warm sunny day.

They got off the truck. Susan thought it was just like being back in England. Susan, Rebecca, Richard and Kevin had decided to go to the top of the rock first. On their way to the cable-car they looked in a few shops, in one of which Rebecca bought a sun-hat. From the lower station of the cable-car they went directly to the upper station at the very top. They got out and explored a bit taking some photographs. After a while they made their way to the café and purchased some snacks and drinks.

'What a lovely day' commented Rebecca, as she sat down.

'The views are tremendous' said Susan, back to her usual self. 'You can see the layout of the harbour and beaches quite clearly.'

'This is the life' said Kevin. 'It's nice to have a day away from the truck.'

Richard had been gazing around as if looking for something. He came over now and put his things on the table then looked for a spare chair. There were two smartly dressed ladies in their late thirties sitting on the next table. They had an extra chair.

'May I?' he said.

'Of course' one of them answered.

He took it and sat down.

'Are you here on holiday?'

'Yes, only it's not really a holiday but an overland tour.'

'Oh, that sounds exciting. So where have you come from and where are you going?'

'Well we started in England and we are heading to Nairobi in Kenya.'

'Fantastic.'

'How about you two?' asked Susan.

'My husband is here on business' said the other lady. 'He is a film director. While he is working we have seized the opportunity for a day out.'

They settled down and ate their snacks.

'So Kevin,' said Rebecca, 'what made you come on this trip?'

'The adventure I guess. I have a small furniture removal business back home in Toronto and it's a bit quiet in the winter months. This year I decided to take six months off and see some of the world.'

'How about you Richard?'

'I was made redundant from my job as a wages clerk. I'd wanted to go to Africa, in particular the jungle, so it was an ideal opportunity.'

'And you Rebecca?'

'I wanted to do a long trip and I am keen to see the wildlife of East Africa therefore this is ideal.'

The two lads turned towards Susan.

'What's your reason for coming?'

'I quit my job at the bank and was at a loose end. I liked various aspects of this tour, crossing the Sahara, seeing the mountain gorillas, and in a reckless moment committed myself for the whole five months.'

'I think you are very brave seeing as you have never camped before' commented Rebecca.

'Haven't you? I agree' added Richard. 'I have at least been on a couple of camping holidays in England.'

'I can't imagine anyone not camping' said Kevin. 'We do it all the time in Canada.'

'Having made the decision I just hoped I would enjoy it' continued Susan 'and thankfully I do.'

An hour or so passed by as they relaxed. They then said goodbye to the two ladies and slowly walked down to see the famous apes, properly called Barbary macaques. From here they took the cable-car to the bottom. Once in town they followed Main Street for a bit. Richard bought some camera film to supplement his stock.

'Ah, there's a large hotel over there' said Susan. 'I want to make a phone call home if I can.'

'That's fine by us, isn't it?' said Rebecca. 'We can hang out in reception while you do.'

'Of course' agreed Kevin.

Richard nodded. He seemed a bit distracted thought Susan. They headed to the hotel and entered. Susan enquired at the reception desk. Yes, said the receptionist, there is a phone in an alcove along the corridor that can be used for an international call. Susan signalled her success to the others and disappeared around the corner. Rebecca, Richard and Kevin sat down on the comfy seats in the foyer.

Susan found the phone, picked up the receiver and dialled the country access code followed by her parent's number. The phone at the other end started to ring. She let it ring ten times before giving up. She looked at her watch. Her father would doubtlessly be at work but her mother would usually be there. Just my luck she thought. This time she tried Kathy's number at work. Again she could hear the phone ringing. On the eighth ring the phone was picked up and a voice on the other end said 'Rainbow Rooms.'

'Kath it's me, Susan. I'm phoning from Gibraltar.'

'Susie', the voice said, 'how are you? How's it going?'

'Good thanks' answered Susan. 'We've got a good group and I am enjoying it.'

'That's great' came the excited reply. 'I'm so glad you rang. You'll never guess what?' Kathy recited the news concerning the park murder. 'And last night on the television they showed a picture of the missing work of art, and it was the tablet. Apparently another art collector in Stockholm has also been recently murdered and a similar tablet was found to be missing from his collection. The police believe there is a connection between the two crimes.' The voice stopped for air.

'Someone tried to snatch my bag in Granada while we were looking around the Alhambra. And,' said Susan, 'I think it is the same tall thin man that you pointed out to me in the car.'

'You're kidding. Oh, nearly forgot. Somebody got into the flat and stole the photo of us at your 31st.'

'Stole our photograph?'

They chatted a bit longer.

'Did you ever find your front door key?'

There was a pause then a reply of, 'no I am still using the spare.'

'Then that's how he got in.'

'Of course, how silly of me not to realise. You be careful Susie.'

'Give my love to my parents when you next speak to them. I tried ringing them but there was no answer.'

'Will do.'

They said their goodbyes and Susan put down the receiver. It was nice to talk to Kathy she thought.

Suddenly from behind a hand came over her mouth and another grabbed her wrist.

'Try to call out and I'll break your arm' a man's voice threatened. 'So Miss Scarlet you have something that I need. Where's the tablet?' He released his hand from her mouth just a little but twisted her wrist making her grimace.

'Somewhere you can't get it' she said defiantly.

'The wrong answer' he said. He part dragged her along the corridor further from reception and twisted her wrist some more. Susan yelped with pain.

'Let's try again shall we. Where is it?'

'It's on the truck.'

'Then you are coming with me to get it off.'

He was pushing her towards a fire exit when Susan heard a familiar voice command, 'Let her go now' followed by a loud shout of 'Kevin.'

Relief flooded through her. With renewed confidence she kicked out with all her might connecting with his shin. He let go of her and was gone through the door just as Kevin appeared.

'You alright' asked Richard, running up to her.

'I am now thanks' she said gratefully.

'You were right' said Kevin.

Half an hour later Susan, Rebecca and Richard were sitting at a table in a nearby pub. Kevin was at the bar ordering a round of drinks. Susan turned to Richard.

'What did Kevin mean when he said you were right?'

'Well, Rebecca told me about your dream last night' Susan looked at Rebecca then back to Richard 'and I reckoned that if this bloke has followed you this far from home he wasn't going to give up that easily. Gibraltar seemed to me to be a good opportunity for him to try again.'

Kevin had returned with a tray of drinks and was sitting down.

'So that's why you have appeared a little distracted today.'

'I must admit I had my doubts' said Kevin 'nevertheless one of us has been keeping an eye on you.'

'Now I understand' Rebecca said to Richard 'why you looked so anxious at the hotel when Susan was out of sight making a phone call.'

'I can't thank you enough' said Susan.
'That's what friends are for' replied Richard.
'Anyhow, I must tell you what Kathy told me over the phone.' She related the latest news to them and they mulled it over while having their drinks.
'This guy isn't going to give up until he gets the tablet' stated Kevin.
'Do you think it is him that wants it or is he working for someone else?' asked Rebecca.
'That's a good question' replied Richard.
'If we could get a copy of it and let him believe he has the real one' Susan hypothesized.
'How are we going to do that?' said Rebecca.
'I have no idea' answered Susan.

Bill had finished reading the newspaper and was preparing to do the crossword when the phone rang.
'Hello – yes, what's the news – okay I see – no, don't do that, concentrate on locating the last tablet for now – let her think you have given up then when her guard is down you can pounce – ring me in a week's time or sooner – bye.'
Bill put the phone down. Incompetent fool he thought. These last few days have not gone well.

That night in the tent Susan was just getting settled in her sleeping bag when Rebecca said softly.
'I think Richard fancies you.'
'Hm. Why do you say that?'
'Intuition.'
'Don't be silly' responded Susan.
Nevertheless she went to sleep with a warm feeling in her heart.

Chapter Nine

Neil drove the truck to the port of Algeciras where they boarded the vehicle ferry. It was a fine day and the crossing to Ceuta only took ninety minutes. During that period Susan, Richard, Rebecca and Kevin kept their eyes open for the tall thin man but he didn't appear to be on board. They were relieved. Colin allowed the group an hour to look around the Spanish enclave before heading to the border. The formalities were completed in an hour. They then drove into Fnideq, the Moroccan border town. Each person had to complete a form stating name, address, nationality, passport number, date and place of issue, length and purpose of visit to the country. Everyone waited quietly in the truck until the border officials were happy that everything was in order. This took about two hours. Watches were then adjusted to coincide with local time. They then drove via M'diq to Tetouan and then finally to Chechaouen where they set up in a campsite in a wooded area, close to a hotel and overlooking the town.

Sitting around the truck after dinner the topic of discussion was their first day in Africa.

'So what do you think of Morocco?' asked Richard.

'I thought the medina in Tetouan was a little scary at first. A bit of a culture shock' replied Susan.

'There were a lot of hustlers. Wonder if we will get that in all the towns' said Rosemary.

'I wasn't sure if they wanted to be our guides or to sell us kef or hashish' commented Louisa.

'Both probably. I expect we will get used to it' said Geoff. 'This town seems more relaxed.'

'I was glad that guy put the snake around Ellie's neck and not mine' grimaced Rosemary. 'I can't stand snakes.'

'I got a good photograph of that' added Susan.

Conversation flowed for a while before people started to retire to their tents for the night. Susan joined Richard as he headed to the sinks to clean his teeth.

'I managed to have a word with Colin' she said. 'I asked him whether it was possible to get a wooden gift made to a specified design for a friend back home, and if so where. He told me it might be possible in Rabat as we had a free day and there were plenty of skilled craftsmen in the medina.'

'You're thinking of getting the tablet copied aren't you?'

'Yes. I am convinced we will see our 'friend' again and I want to be ready when we do. He won't give up yet, I just know it.'

'What if he realises it is a copy?'

'I don't think he will. I believe he is acting on behalf of someone else.'

'I hope you are right.'

'So will you come with me when we get to Rabat?' asked Susan.

Richard looked at her then grinned.

'How's your French?'

'Il est tres bon' she replied.

'D'accord, pas de problème.'

'Merci' she smiled.

The next day passed pleasantly. The highlight was a tour of the ruins of Volubilis, a town once inhabited by the Romans nearly two thousand years earlier. The other item that found its way into Susan's diary was the campsite. It would be their home for two nights and was situated in a wooded area outside of Fes. The toilet and shower block was shared by both sexes and was located on the other side of a small lake reached by way of a flat wooden bridge. There were no doors on the cubicles, only ill-fitting plastic curtains. It was a dirty and smelly building in contrast to the pretty campsite.

The town of Fes consists of three parts; the new town, the royal city and mellah or Jewish quarter, and the medina. The group were driven to the royal city where they saw the outstanding brass doors of the Royal Palace. Colin then hired a guide to lead them on a tour of the medina.

The guide entered the medina at the gate of Bab Bou Jeloud then after a quick left and right headed down Talaa Kebira Street. The route he took led them past the Bou Inania Medressa, the Kairaouine Mosque, the souks and the tanneries. The medina was a twisting maze of alleyways with heavily laden mules trying to get a grip on the well-worn paths. The tour ended in a carpet shop owned by a brother of the guide.

Heading back to the campsite most of the group decided to try a hammam or steam bath. There was a separate side for men and women.

That evening Susan was sitting around the camp fire chatting.

'I can see why Colin hired us a guide' Rebecca was saying. 'I would never have found my way back out again.'

'Yes it was confusing' agreed Rosemary.

'I thought the most interesting place were the tanneries' said Susan. 'They were a bit smelly though.'

'Did you know they use cow urine to process the skins' explained Richard.

'That's disgusting' interjected Rebecca.

'And pigeon droppings apparently' he continued.

'They use natural dyes such as saffron and indigo to get the colours' added Susan.

'I enjoyed the hammam the best' said Rebecca, changing the subject. 'I had a great massage. It was quite a surprise to see all the local women stripped off and naked.'

'Oh. In the men's side things were much more modest as everyone wore underpants.'

'Boring' said Rosemary.

'It was a lot nicer washing in the hammam than here, that's for sure' commented Susan.

They arrived in Rabat late afternoon on the following day, staying in a campsite in the neighbouring town of Sale. The campsite had the usual facilities plus a shop. It was situated at the top of a beach and was fenced in and guarded at all times.

Susan and Richard were up in good time and discussed their plans over breakfast.

'Colin says if we go to the Rue des Consuls in the medina we should be able to find a craftsman that can help us.' She showed Richard on the map. 'The area is relatively free of hassle and the traders are quite trustworthy.'

'Have you got the tablet on you?'

'Yes. Rebecca gave it to me earlier. It's in my bag. I have arranged a time and meeting place with her for lunch.'

'Let's hope it all goes smoothly.'

After breakfast Colin handed out visa application forms for Burkina Faso and Chad. He explained that the ones for Chad would only be required if they were unable to obtain visas for Nigeria. Once completed he collected them back up again together with their passports. He would collect the visas later in the day.

Not long afterwards Neil drove the truck into Rabat and dropped everyone at one corner of the medina.

'I believe we are quite close to the street Colin suggested' Susan said optimistically.

'I do too' agreed Richard. 'I reckon it's straight ahead then first on the right.'

They walked forward and soon came upon a road full of artisan shops.

'This looks promising.'

They gazed briefly into a few shops until coming to one that had a selection of wooden souvenirs.

'I'll ask at this one' said Susan.

They entered and Susan went up to the person in charge.

'Bonjour' she said then in her best French 'we wish to get an item made in wood, is it possible that you can help us?'

'No, we do not make wooden artefacts here, but maybe my friend along the street can help you.'

He gave them directions. Further into the medina they asked again only to get the same reply and new directions. This occurred on two more occasions.

'I think we are on a wild goose chase' remarked Richard despondently.

'Let's not give up yet' encouraged Susan. 'We knew it wouldn't be easy.'

They found the next shop and repeated their request.

'What is it that you want made?' asked the shopkeeper.

Susan got out the tablet and showed him.

'We would like to get a copy of this if it is possible, only we leave tomorrow morning.'

The shopkeeper looked at it with interest.

'Where did you get this?'

'A friend in London gave it to me.'

'And you knew to come to me?'

'No' explained Richard. 'This is the fifth place we have enquired at this morning.'

'It is curious because I believe my uncle has the very same piece.'

'Your uncle? Does he live here in Rabat?' asked Susan.

'Yes he does. Maybe you would like to meet him. I think he is looking to sell it.' Susan looked at Richard who shrugged then nodded.

'Okay; but are you able to make a copy of this one, and how much would you charge?'

'You give me little time but perhaps it is possible. It will not be very expensive.'

He called out in Arabic and a boy about fifteen years old appeared. He said a few words to him and then turned to Richard.

'My grandson will guide you. My uncle lives in the Kasbah, not too far away. I will need to keep this' he held up the tablet 'so that I can get the detail correct.'

Susan looked apprehensive.

'Do not worry my friend for it is safe with me. Now go.'

Susan hesitated briefly then turned and the two of them followed the boy. They walked through the medina. Susan suddenly grabbed Richards arm and pointed.

'Look!' she said in a loud whisper. 'It's him.'

Richard stared ahead just in time to see a familiar figure disappear into a shop.

'What's he doing here I wonder?'

'He is surely not buying souvenirs' replied Richard.

They left the medina, crossed the road and entered the Kasbah at the enormous gate of Bab Oudaia. The boy turned this way then that, leading them finally to a whitewashed property.

'Wait here' said the boy.

He went inside and they heard him talk to someone in Arabic. The door opened again.

'Follow me' he said.

They entered. It was cooler inside and the rooms were ornately furnished. It reminded Susan of a museum or maybe a stately home but on a much smaller scale. They were led into a courtyard where an old man was sitting. He turned towards them.

'Come' he beckoned. 'Sit down. You will have some tea?'

He gave commands to the boy who hurried off. 'He tells me that you are interested in a piece of art that I own. I will show you it later but first I wish to ask you a few questions. Where do you come from?'

'We come from England' answered Richard.

'And why do you visit my country?'

'We are on a long journey through Africa' said Susan. 'Our destination is Nairobi in Kenya and this is the first country of many that we shall be visiting.'

'Do you have your own vehicle?'

'No' she replied 'we are touring with an overland company and it is their vehicle that we are travelling in. It is a large truck and there are 20 other people on the trip.'

'I used to travel once when I was younger. Now it is not possible.'

He stopped talking as the young lad had returned with a tray containing a pot of mint tea and three small glasses.

'Come, we will have some tea.'

He signalled to the boy who filled the three glasses and departed.

'Please.'

He handed a glass to each of them.

'Thank you' they said.

The three of them drank the warm sweet liquid.

'That is better' said the old man. 'There is plenty. Pour yourself another.'

'Have you always collected artefacts' asked Susan.

'Once I was a business man then when I retired I bought some pieces that interested me. It is but a hobby. When you have finished your tea I will show you.'

Twenty minutes later they left the courtyard and followed the old man into an adjoining room. There were many fine examples of ceramics, most with geometric designs. He opened the drawer of a desk and took out a wooden tablet.

'Is this the item you are interested in?'

He handed it to Richard.

'Incredible.'

He flipped it over to look at the other side then passed it to Susan. She gazed at it in amazement.

'It's the same as the one I have.'

'You have a piece like this?' asked the old man.

'Yes, although the symbols differ.'

'I always wondered if it was unique or part of something bigger. As you see I mainly collect ceramics but this always intrigued me so I kept it.'

'My piece intrigues me also. Where did you get this one?'

'I bought it in Paris many moons ago.' There was silence. 'Maybe you would like to buy it?'

'Only if you wish to sell' said Susan.

The old man studied her and Richard in turn. He was quiet as he mulled it over in his mind. Finally he spoke.

'I have come to a decision' he said. 'I have had this piece for all these years and have never discovered what it is. I could ask you for money but I am in my 88th year and what I yearn for more is to know if it has a meaning and if so what that meaning is. You are good people I can tell; therefore I will give this to you on the condition that if you are able to find out for me this meaning then that will be recompense enough.'

'I cannot take it for nothing' said Susan a little startled.

'Nonsense my child. I will give you my address and when you have news write to me. I have only a few years left so do not take too long.'

It was now Susan's turn to contemplate what she should do. She reached a decision.

'Okay' she said 'I will do as you ask. I cannot promise I will be successful but whatever I might find out I will inform you.'

'Thank you. I am sorry. I do not know your names.'

'Susan Scarlet.'

'And Richard Newman.'

'And what is your name?' asked Susan.

'Malik al Mansour.'

The young lad led them out of the Kasbah and back to the Rue des Consuls. He then slipped away into the medina. Susan looked at her watch. It was twenty five past twelve.

'I told Rebecca that we would meet her at twelve thirty at the drop off point. It's nearly that time now.'

'Let's hurry then. We won't be too late.'

They rushed as best they could through the busy streets arriving about ten minutes after the meeting time. She wasn't there.

'I guess we missed her.'

'Never mind. Let's find a café and eat. I'm hungry' said Susan.

They started to walk away when a familiar voice called out. They turned to see Kevin and Rebecca heading towards them.

'I bet you thought you had missed us' said Kevin.

'Yes we did' replied Richard.

'So how did your morning go?' asked Rebecca.

'Okay. I'll tell you all about it once we have found a café' replied Susan.

They found somewhere nearby and ordered lunch.

'Come on Susan; spill the beans' begged Rebecca, eagerly awaiting the news.

'Well we found a man that can make a copy of the tablet.'

'That's great' commented Rebecca.

Susan glanced at Richard then continued.

'And his uncle gave me a souvenir; another tablet.'

'Come again' said Kevin.

'You're joking!' responded Rebecca.

Susan told them of their visit to the shop and to the house in the Kasbah.

'Wow, you have had an exciting morning' said Rebecca.

'Oh, I nearly forgot, we also saw our 'friend' shopping in the medina.'

'Him again' said Kevin. 'That's bad news.'

'So can we see the new tablet?' asked Rebecca.

'I don't wish to show you here. There will be plenty of time to study it when we get back to the safety of the campsite. Only I would like one of you to take care of it till then.'

'I'll take care of it' said Kevin.

'Thanks.'

Susan passed him the tablet wrapped in a tissue. Kevin took it and zipped it up in his trouser pocket. Their food arrived soon after.

'Have you seen all the spices in the market?' Rebecca said to Susan.

'No, I haven't.'

'I'll show you after lunch. They are so colourful.'

They stayed together until four o'clock when Susan and Richard headed back to the shop.

'Do you know the way?' asked Susan.

'I think so, providing we follow the same route as we took earlier.'

Twenty minutes later they reached their destination. The shopkeeper wasn't to be seen but the young lad that had guided them earlier was there. He beckoned them to sit down. He then disappeared into a back room and presently returned with his grandfather.

'Good, you are here. Did you reach a deal with my uncle?'

'Yes' replied Susan.

'Excellent. I have managed to make a copy of the piece for you.' He went behind a desk and produced two items, the original and the copy. 'Please.' He gave the pieces to Susan. 'I have used cedar wood. The edges were difficult to replicate and the symbols do not have the same intensity but I have done the best that I can.'

Susan studied the copy and compared it to the original.

'You have made a good job of it. That should do the trick. It is strange though that although they look similar they feel quite different somehow.'

'I thought the same' he said.

Susan passed them to Richard.

'Yes I see what you mean. The real one is a little heavier.' He balanced it on his finger. 'Maybe I am imagining it but the centre of it seems denser.'

'How much do I owe you?' asked Susan.

They settled on a price and Susan handed over the money. She then handed the real tablet to Richard for safekeeping and she put the copy in her bag.

'Merci beaucoup. Au revoir.'

They were about to leave when Richard stopped her.

'Look, further down the street.'

'What, oh I see.' She thought for a moment then added 'I believe it is time to set my plan into action.'

Before Richard could stop her she had gone, walking in a carefree manner straight towards the tall thin man.

Chapter Ten

The shopkeeper had come to stand beside Richard.
'Is there a problem?' he asked.
Richard explained the situation as briefly as possible.
'I will send my grandson to keep watch from a distance. That way he will not suspect anything.'
He called to the back of the shop and the boy appeared. Further commands and the boy left the shop.
Matt looked ahead to see Susan walking in his direction. Well, well he thought; if it isn't our Miss Scarlet and she appears to be alone. It's my lucky day. He waited till she was close and then came up beside her locking his arm through hers.
'No heroics and you won't get hurt' he hissed. She looked at him fearfully. 'Not so brave now are we without your friends around.'
Susan kept quiet and meekly went with him. He led her along a couple of streets and far into a back alleyway. There was nobody about.
'So Miss Scarlet. Where is it?'
'I don't know what you mean' she replied.
'Oh I think you do. Now where is the tablet?' She deliberately held her bag tightly to her body and said nothing. 'Is it in there?' he asked. He looked at her. 'It is isn't it?'
'No' she said unconvincingly.
'Open it' he ordered, squeezing her arm extremely tightly.

'Let go, you're hurting me.'

'When I have what I want' he replied.

'Okay. If I give you the tablet will you leave me alone?' begged Susan.

'Now you are being sensible.'

Susan opened her bag and extracted the tablet. He snatched it from her hand, glanced at it and put it in his pocket. Good he's taken the bait thought Susan.

'Well done. That wasn't too difficult now was it?' he said condescendingly. He had liked the feel of her close to him. His thoughts turned to other things. 'We could have some fun you and me.' He held her tightly and kissed her lips against her will. Susan shuddered. His breath smelt of cigarettes and alcohol. She had expected him to go once he had the tablet. She hadn't planned for this. She was starting to get scared. 'That was nice wasn't it?'

'No' said Susan bluntly.

'Feisty aren't we' he smirked. 'I like a girl who is hard to get. All the more fun when I do.'

He rotated her so that he was behind her and put his hand down her blouse, feeling the warmth of her breasts through her bra. He was getting excited. He could feel an erection building.

Susan felt terrified. She struggled as best as she could but he was strong and held her too tightly. His hand was now trying to grope her lower down. What can I do to stop him she thought? Suddenly there was activity along the alley. Two people had started to run towards her. She realised that she was no longer being held. Clutching her bag she ran to them.

Richard reached her first and held her in his arms. She was trembling.

'You're safe now' he said soothingly.

The young lad was there also. He guided them back to the shop.

A short distance away Matt was thinking what a pity. He would have enjoyed having her. Never mind, the main thing is he had the tablet and there were always more girls to be had.

They were in the shop and Susan was drinking a cup of sweet mint tea. She had regained her composure.

'Don't ever do that again' scolded Richard. She looked at him warmly.

'Sorry but I wanted the meeting to be as realistic as possible and not give him any reason for doubts. I never dreamt it would turn out like that.'

'Please, just be more careful in future. I was really worried.' She squeezed his hand.

'It worked anyhow. He never suspected anything. Maybe now he will leave me alone. Don't worry, I've learnt from my mistake. I won't underestimate strangers again, I promise.'

It was getting late. They had to be back in the campsite soon. The shopkeeper suggested that they take a rowboat from near the Kasbah straight to Sale. The young lad led them the quick way to it.

'Thanks Ahmed' Susan said to the young lad. 'We are very grateful for all your help.'

'It was no trouble mademoiselle' replied the young lad.

They took the row boat across the river. As they walked towards the campsite Susan said to Richard,

'Please don't tell the others the full story.'

'It's okay, I won't. I don't want to embarrass you.'

'Thanks' she replied, smiling.

That evening Susan, Rebecca, Richard and Kevin were

sitting down chatting. Rebecca was questioning Susan on the events of the afternoon and Susan had told her everything up to and including the handing over of the copy.

'Well done' Rebecca said, 'you were brave. Didn't you feel nervous; I know I would have done?'

'Only a little bit' she answered. Her eyes met Richard who winked knowingly.

'Let's have a look at the new tablet' said Kevin.

'Okay.'

Susan took it out of her bag and passed it around. They each looked at it in turn and then passed it back to her. She had taken out her notepad and now set about deciphering the runes.

'We have an l, s, o, u, ng, n and d with number values of 22, 16, 23, 2, 21, 24 and 10' she said.

They all wrote the details down on pieces of paper.

'I see the middle letter is also a rune this time.'

Richard had written the numbers down in numerical order (2, 10, 16, 21, 22, 23, and 24).

'I see that four of the numbers follow in sequence. Which runes are those?' asked Richard.

Susan pointed them out on the tablet.

'So maybe it is the other three that are important' stated Rebecca.

They all looked at her disbelievingly.

'What?' Unfazed she continued with her theory. 'And that gives us s, u, n, sun. There we are.'

The other three stared at her in amazement.

'I do believe you're on to something' said Kevin in support.

'Thanks.'

'The unknown symbol on the first tablet reminded me of the sun' said Susan, 'so perhaps you are right.'

'We know there are at least three of these tablets and as

they are hexagonal I reckon there must be seven of them in all' said Richard.

'Why seven?' asked Rebecca.

'One in the middle and six around the outside.'

'Oh, okay. Sorry I'm not very good with figures.'

'If what you say is correct Richard' said Kevin, 'I wonder if one of these is the middle one.'

Susan put one piece on the table and went to align the other one beside it, but the two pieces repelled each other.

'I think they are magnetic' said Susan surprised.

'Try it against the other sides' suggested Richard.

Susan did just that. She discovered that every other side repelled or attracted.

'How odd. Normally a magnet has one north and one south pole. These seem to have three. Unless of course each tablet contains three tiny magnets.'

'Or even six' added Susan.

'At least this reduces the odds of how to place the two pieces together; before there were thirty six possibilities whereas now there are nine.'

'I'll take your word on that' said Rebecca bemused.

'Maybe only three' said Susan 'for if my notion is correct the first tablet is the central one. Do you see how the runes circle the unknown symbol in the middle? Well it would make sense if the runes on the outer tablets did likewise.'

'So which one of the three sides would it be?' pondered Richard out loud.

Susan aligned the tablets in each of the probable positions but they couldn't decide which one was correct. No new ideas were forthcoming so Susan put the two tablets back in her bag. A few minutes later Chris and Louisa came over.

'Hi. Any of you up for a game of cards?' asked Louisa.

'Yeh, sure' said Kevin.

'Yes okay' agreed the others.

He had dialled the number and was now waiting to be connected. Finally the phone rang and Bill answered.

'Hi, it's Matt – Rabat – yes – I have Miss Scarlet's tablet and I know where the other one is – thanks – I will get it tomorrow – okay – about a week I expect – bye.'

He hung up. It's been a good day thought Matt; maybe I'll have a wee drink before I go to bed.

Chapter Eleven

It was midday when Matt entered the Kasbah. He managed to negotiate the maze of streets to find the whitewashed property he sought. He knocked the door and waited. There was no immediate answer. He tried the door and it opened. Once inside he closed the door and looked around; very decorative he thought. He was about to venture further when he heard someone approaching. It was an old man.

'Are you Mr Mansour?' asked Matt.

'That is correct.'

'I believe you have an item of art that I wish to buy.'

'Come, we will go to the courtyard. There is more air there.'

The old man led the way and Matt followed. Once in the courtyard the old man sat down and beckoned Matt to do likewise but he remained standing. The old man was silent.

'I am looking for a wooden tablet with symbols on it. I understand that you have such a piece.'

'Who told you that?'

'It doesn't matter. Do you have it?'

'Perhaps I know of the piece, but why do you want to buy it?'

'That is my business.'

'And what would you give me for this piece?'

'Five hundred dirham.'

The old man studied the tall thin man for a while.

'So will you sell?'

'That is not possible.'

'I will double the amount but that is my final offer.'

'That is very generous however your money does not interest me.'

'Then you give me no alternative' said Matt threateningly.

'You misunderstand me. I cannot sell you the piece because it is no longer in my possession.'

'What? So who did you sell it to?'

'I do not know for I did not enquire of their names' he lied.

'When did you sell it?'

'Yesterday, for a price that was more rewarding to me than your offer.'

Matt considered for a minute; surely it wasn't Miss Scarlet and one of her friends. No that would be impossible.

'Were they English?'

'They spoke in French' answered the old man.

Matt cursed. He turned and stormed out of the house.

The old man sat quietly thinking. I did well to give it to the young couple. That man is a dangerous fool.

The town of Marrakech consists of two parts; the new town and the medina. On the Monday the group had a full day to see the place. Caleches (horse drawn cabs) and a guide were hired for a tour of the medina. Susan shared a cab with Rebecca. It was an interesting ride. The guide took them to the Dar Si-Said, housing the Museum of Moroccan Arts, El Bahia, the former palace of the sultan and his harem, the Saadian tombs, and the souks. They then had some free time in the afternoon before heading to the main square of Djemaa el Fna in the evening. Colin advised them not to take cameras but just take in the sights and sounds. Susan could feel the electric atmosphere as soon as she arrived.

Within the square there were acrobats, comedians, dancers, fire-eaters, musicians, snake-charmers, storytellers (some in drag), water sellers, a dentist with a display of molars, and an herbalist selling dubious looking concoctions. People were selling their wares neatly laid out on the ground. Children begged for sweets, pens and money. Stalls, lit by lanterns at twilight, were selling freshly squeezed orange and lime juice plus all manner of things to eat. A gambling game was taking place with the winner decided by the roll of the die. Susan was so captivated by it all that she had forgotten all about the tall thin man. Richard however was alert and stayed close to her at all times. Thankfully he didn't see him in the crowds. It seemed that Susan's ruse had worked.

The next day they drove south to Imlil. Colin hired a guide and two mules for the two-day trek up Mount Toubkal in the High Atlas Mountains. They would depart the next morning. They drove back down the road and camped in a field of grass by a stream.

Morning dawned and Neil drove them back to Imlil. The two mules were loaded up with the food supplies and the group's sleeping bags. They were led along the easier but longer track on the west side of the valley while the group followed the shorter track on the east. An hour later they arrived at the village of Aremd, built on a spur of rocks above the Mizane valley, a very fertile area with terraced fields of maize, potato, onion, barley and various fruits when in season. There was also grazing for cattle and goats.
    The guide lived in Aremd and he invited everyone into his home. Susan climbed the narrow flight of stairs to the first floor. Here there was a stone balcony and they were served with thé a la menthe by the guide's wife. Outside

in the narrowest of streets some villagers were singing and dancing.

'What's the matter?' said Susan to Richard who was rubbing his forehead.

'I just cracked my head against the stone lintel as I entered the house. It's such a low doorway.'

'You okay?'

'Yes, I'll be fine, thanks. I'm just a little dazed that's all.'

'This sweet tea will bring you round.'

'Sometimes it is an advantage being short' said Rebecca. 'I walked under it without bending my head.'

An hour passed and then the group carried on walking to the next village of Sidi Chamharouch. It was a tiny place with a seasonal population that ran several provisions shops. They stopped for lunch.

At one o'clock the group took the trail which continued above the course of the Midane River. The path was covered with loose scree of volcanic origin. Udo set the pace with Richard and Susan following and the others a little further behind.

'You've done this before haven't you?' said Richard to Udo.

'Of course, I walk a lot at home. How about you?'

'Yes, I like to get out when I get the chance.'

'I wish I was as fit as you two' said Susan, puffing a little.

'I think you are doing fine' said Richard.

'I like walking but haven't done much lately.'

'Come, we will stop to drink' said Udo.

This they did. Although they were sweating from the climb the wind had turned chilly and they put on more clothing. They carried on, reaching the refuge hut at Neltner by three o'clock. The mules arrived soon after and the three of them helped unload them and carry the gear inside.

The hut contained a sink, a stove, table and benches. The

sleeping quarters were upstairs and the toilet was outside. There was no running water or heating.

'Just our luck to be on cooking duties today and tomorrow' said Richard, looking around and finding that they were alone for a minute.

'Never mind, it will be an experience' replied Susan.

'What did you do with the tablets? Did you leave them in the truck?'

'No. They are in my bag. As we won't see the truck for two days I decided it would be better to bring them with me where I could keep an eye on them.'

Richard considered the situation then said, 'I believe you did the right thing. There is only Colin and Alison to watch the truck. Our 'friend' could well find a way on board.'

'Don't worry. I don't think he will be bothering us in the near future.'

The rest of the group arrived in dribs and drabs. Susan, Richard and Louisa prepared and cooked dinner a little earlier than usual. This was devoured with relish as everyone was hungry after the climb. Once the washing up was completed they all sat around the table and chatted. A few of the group played cards for a while but as there was only an oil lamp to provide light many drifted off to bed for an early night.

'Hey, I thought we would have beds but it's just one large sleeping area' said Susan.

'Yes. It's like being in a can of sardines' agreed Rebecca.

'No turning over then' joked Rosemary 'or we will all have to.'

Richard, Louisa and the guide were the last to retire. Richard used the toilet before doing so and noticed a few flakes of snow were falling.

When they got up in the morning they found that there had been a blizzard in the night which had deposited a couple of feet of snow on the ground. They had planned to climb to the summit first thing but the guide said it would not be possible. Susan was secretly pleased. She hadn't been looking forward to scrambling up a mountain at six thirty in the morning and now was glad she didn't have to.

The group set out at nine o'clock for the descent. The mules had returned to Imlil the previous afternoon so everyone had more luggage to carry. The going was slow owing to the depth of the snow.

'Lovely blue sky' said Kevin. 'It's just like being home in the winter.'

'Yes it's a beautiful day, so tranquil' agreed Susan. 'I just wish I had my boots with me.'

'Likewise' said Richard who was slipping and sliding in all directions.

'I just never imagined that it might snow' continued Susan. 'It's been sunny now for weeks.'

'Help!' cried Rebecca who had found another deep patch of snow. 'I take back what I said yesterday about the advantage of being short.'

Kevin hauled her up.

'It's a shame we have missed out on the summit' commented Richard.

'I agree. I was looking forward to that' said Kevin.

'Am I the only one who is glad not to have had to climb a mountain so early in the day?' remarked Susan.

She never got a reply as at that moment Richard slipped and went head first into the snow.

'That was so funny' laughed Rebecca.

The other two chuckled also and finally Kevin helped him up.

'Were you looking for a short cut' added Rebecca, who burst out laughing again.

'Very funny' said Richard smiling. He had now seen the amusing side of it.

They plodded on, eventually reaching Sidi Chamharouch. The snow was less deep on the trail to Aremd and had turned to streams of water by the time they got to Imlil.

Susan sought out Alison.

'How have things been with you?' she asked.

'Relaxing. It was good to have a couple of days off.'

'Nothing unusual happened then?'

'No. All very peaceful.'

Just as I had expected thought Susan as she walked away to find Richard. No tall thin man obviously snooping around. We won't be seeing him again.

Chapter Twelve

It was on the Monday, a week after leaving Marrakech, when Matt finally arrived in London. It had been an exhausting drive. He didn't go to Bill's but instead returned to his apartment, picking up a takeaway, some beer and a packet of his favourite tobacco on the way. Bill can wait till tomorrow he thought. Tonight I am having a lazy evening at home in front of the television.

Bill was sitting at his desk munching a custard cream. Matt had just recounted the story of his time in Rabat and was now standing up gazing out of the window. When Matt had handed over the tablet Bill had put it in the drawer of his desk. He had seemed more interested in the missing seventh piece than with obtaining the sixth.
  'Weren't you able to find out whether the seventh piece is still in Rabat?'
  'I told you. I made dozens of enquiries but drew a blank. It seems to have disappeared without trace.'
  'Inconceivable.'
  Matt returned to his chair and started to roll a cigarette. Bill took another biscuit from the packet and munched on it contentedly. Matt lit his cigarette.
  Once Matt had departed Bill opened the drawer of his desk and took out the latest tablet. It appeared to be the central one, the most important of them all. Excellent he thought. He then went over to his bed and opened a

concealed unit underneath it, taking out the other five tablets. These he carried over to the desk and arranged them around the new tablet. They fitted snugly and yet something was wrong. The new central tablet wasn't being attracted to the others as he had expected. He tried it in a different position but there was no change. That can't be right he reasoned. He picked it up and studied it. It felt lighter than the others. The runes, although bright, didn't shine so powerfully.

He rubbed it between his fingers; was he imagining it or had his fingers discoloured. He looked at the tablet again. A very slight blemish had appeared on it. I knew it he said to himself, this tablet is a fake.

Two hours later Matt answered the phone.

'Where have you been? – never mind, I want you to call round straight away – that doesn't matter – today, now.'

Bill put down the receiver. He didn't get angry very often but just now he was livid.

Now who's rattled his cage thought Matt as he moved away from the phone. Guess I had better get going. He left the flat, slammed the door and got in his car.

When Matt entered the flat Bill was drinking a cup of tea.

'Sit down.'

Matt did as he was instructed.

'This latest tablet is a fake.'

Bill slapped it down on the desk.

'That can't be.'

'Well I am telling you it is nothing but a worthless copy.'

Matt was about to speak but changed his mind. He recalled the day he took it from Miss Scarlet. Her actions had been natural enough although he had expected her to put up more of a fight. Surely she hadn't planned the whole thing but then what other explanation could there be.

'The sneaky bitch' he said finally. 'She must have slipped me a copy and kept the real one.'

'It seems this Miss Scarlet is cleverer than you thought and has outwitted you. Maybe she has the other tablet as well.'

'If she has she will pay for it. I'll teach her to make a fool out of me.'

The group had just crossed from Morocco into Algeria and were waiting patiently at the border post for the formalities to be completed. It was a long wait. For something to do Susan was updating the route on her map.

'Where did we go after the trek up Mount Toubkal?' she asked Richard.

'Back to Marrakech. Then we followed this road' he pointed it out on the map 'via Ouarzazate, Todrha, Er Rachidia, Boudnib and Bouarfa.'

'Thanks. I liked Todrha. I thought the gorge was great. I also enjoyed seeing the oases at Tinerhir and Meski.'

'It made a change staying at the hotel in Todrha and not having to put up a tent.'

'And to eat in the restaurant.'

'And watching Rebecca and Barbara's interpretation of the 'dance of the seven veils'; highly entertaining.'

'Yes, Morocco has been great; accept for a certain incident of course. I wonder what Algeria will be like?'

Eventually, after having their luggage checked and Colin giving the officials some tins of meat and jam as a bribe, they were allowed to enter the country. It had taken six and a half hours; eight and a half including the two hours on the Moroccan side. Consequently, as it was getting late, they camped close to the perimeter fence.

Once dinner had been eaten Colin called a meeting to discuss security. He told the group that for the rest of the tour each of the six cooking teams would be called upon to do guard duty as and when it was necessary. The duties would be worked in half-hourly or hourly shifts. Also two members of the cooking crew would be required to sleep on the truck.

A week went by during which time they visited Algiers and Ghardaia. That evening they camped in a vast expanse of sand dunes to the north of El Golea. Colin called another meeting after dinner. On this occasion the subject was crossing the Sahara Desert. He impressed upon the group that water might be difficult to come by so the use of it, other than for drinking, would be restricted. Only two litres per person would be allowed for personal washing. Any excess water left over from the cooking would be recycled for washing-up. These measures would enable them to travel for three days without fresh supplies, for five days if they ceased to wash.

As the meeting finished Richard turned to Susan.

'Do you fancy having a look at the stars? I have a star chart in my locker.'

'Yes, that would be great. I've always wanted to learn the constellations but have never got around to it.'

Richard went to the truck and returned with the chart and his torch. They walked away from the lights of the truck, into the desert.

'Isn't it amazing how many stars are visible out here?' commented Susan. 'Sometimes I can barely see any at home.'

They sat on the edge of a dune and Richard explained how to use the planisphere.

'The stars you see in the sky depend on three things; the latitude you are at, the date, and the time. This chart is for latitude 23½, or the Tropic of Cancer. We are a little north of there but it is close enough. Now today is the 2nd of December and the time is 21:30, so you set one against the other like so.' He moved the outer disc so that the two measurements coincided. 'The stars that are visible are the ones shown here.' He pointed to the section of stars showing through the clear plastic on the planisphere.

'Okay, I follow that.'

'So now we can use the chart to read what we can see in the night sky. Do you see the fuzzy band of stars crossing the sky?'

'Yes, I see them.'

'Well that's the Milky Way.' He indicated their position on the planisphere.

'Right.'

'Now can you see four bright stars with three more crossing through the centre?' He pointed towards them.

'I think so.'

'That is the constellation of Orion. The bright star to the east is Sirius the brightest in the sky, and looking to the other side we have Aldebaran in the constellation of Taurus.'

Susan looked up at the sky, then at the chart, then back again towards the sky. Slowly she worked out the position of the brighter stars.

'What's that bright one there?' asked Susan pointing.

'That's Jupiter. Planets don't feature on the chart as their positions change all the time.'

She gazed skyward again. 'And those near the bright star in Taurus?' Richard tried to work out which stars she was looking at. 'I think there are seven of them all close together.'

'Oh that is the Pleiades.'

Susan studied them and the others close by. They somehow seemed familiar. Where had she seen them recently? She suddenly remembered.

'Those stars there in Taurus, they look very similar to the stars on the second tablet.'

'Really' said Richard. 'I must confess I didn't take much notice of the side with the stars on. Tomorrow we must compare the tablet and the chart.'

They gazed upwards.

'Do you know it's nearly ten thirty' said Susan glancing at her watch. 'We had better get back before the lights go out.'

They walked back to the truck.

'Thanks. I've enjoyed my first lesson.'

'Just say when you are ready for lesson two.'

Susan entered the tent to find Rebecca already tucked up in her sleeping bag.

'Where have you been?' she enquired inquisitively.

'I was looking at the stars with Richard.'

'Are you sure it was the stars you were looking at?'

Susan blushed but the darkness in the tent concealed her embarrassment.

'Stop it you' she said happily. 'You're as bad as Kathy.'

The following day was a busy one and comparing the tablet with the star chart was soon forgotten. In the morning they were in the town of El Golea. While there they visited a church, the cemetery of which contained the tomb of the French missionary and explorer Charles de Foucauld. In the afternoon they drove south. The land became flatter and stonier until there was nothing to see on the horizon. Eventually they left the main road and followed the piste (rough track) to Fort Mirabell, a deserted foreign legion fort. The going was slow and bumpy. Dust and sand sprayed up in all directions settling in a thick film on the ledges inside the truck. It was two hours before they arrived. The skeleton of a dead camel lay by the road close to the entrance.

The fort was duly explored. Within the walls was a central square with a row of dormitories along either side. The rooms at the far end appeared to have been used for storage and one had probably been the kitchen. Although the place had long since been deserted there was evidence of it having been used by other travellers. There were the remains of fires and considerable amounts of litter, in particular empty bottles.

That night Susan, Rebecca, Richard and Kevin decided to sleep within the walls of the fort. They selected a dormitory on merit and swept it clean of dust and dirt. Sleeping mats were laid on the stone floor and sleeping bags were unrolled upon these. They lit a mosquito coil to provide some light.

'This is good fun' commented Kevin. 'We have camped in some interesting spots but this is the most atmospheric.'

'Yes, this is great' agreed Rebecca.

'What is everyone's most memorable highlight so far? Mine is coming here.'

'The market in Ghardaia.'

'The square of Djemaa el Fna in Marrakech' said Susan, trying to forget her escapade in Rabat. 'There was so much going on.'

'I enjoyed the trek up Mount Toubkal' added Richard.

'And what about everyone's worst moment on the truck' asked Rebecca.

'Washing-up without a doubt' said Richard instantly. 'Thankfully it is only two days in every twelve.'

'Using the diesel cooker' said Kevin. 'It is so filthy. I shall be glad when we can cook on an open fire.'

'Definitely not as bad as sharing a tent with Rebecca' suggested Susan, with a big grin on her face as she avoided a prod in the ribs, 'but seriously it is finding a loo spot when we are rough camping in areas with little vegetation.'

'Mine was the drive along that bumpy road getting here,

and also all the dust. I will be glad when we don't have restrictions on water use.'

It went quiet.

'Who can do shadow puppets?' asked Rebecca.

They amused themselves for a while longer before finally going to sleep.

Bill reached for the phone and dialled Matt's number.

'Hi it's Bill – we are going to Paris and then Mali in Africa – as soon as possible – I'll see you at the airport tomorrow – and dispose of anything in your flat that can be connected to Africa, the tablets or the flat here – bye.'

Bill put down the receiver. He got up from the desk, walked over to his bed and took out the five tablets from the secret compartment underneath it. He put them, together with the fake piece, into a soft pouch that he wore under his jumper. Next he unzipped a large holdall and into it packed a change of clothes and his washing kit from the bathroom. Taking the holdall over to the desk he emptied the contents of the drawer into it as well. Looking around the flat he checked that no incriminating evidence had been left. Once satisfied he put on his hat and coat and left the flat locking the door behind him. If the police do manage to track down this place he thought, it will do them no good.

Another five days passed by. The journey took the group through the oasis town of In Salah, Arak Gorge where they saw thousand year old engravings of elephants on the rocks, In Ecker and eventually to Tamanrasset.

The first poste restante of the tour was here so many of the group were excited by the prospect of getting mail.

Susan searched through the letters and found two addressed to her; one from her parents and one from Kathy.

She would read them later when she had some free time.

Visa application forms were filled out for Mali and Niger. The Niger visas, Colin explained, just like the Chad ones, would only be used if they were unable to obtain visas for Nigeria.

They stayed at a campsite containing toilets, showers, sinks, a café and a restaurant. The large site had one tree-lined road that led to the restaurant. There were a couple of other overland vehicles in the camp.

After lunch Susan opened the two letters she had received. The first one was from her parents. It was mostly family news. It made her feel a little homesick. She then opened the second one. This one was from Kathy. Her news was upbeat and jovial. It mentioned her work in the café and mutual friends. The letter then concluded thus.

> The local murder and the one in
> Stockholm have both featured in the news.
> The two countries police forces are
> collaborating over the deaths and the
> significance of the tablets.
> I reported finding your tablet to the
> police. Barry, a customer, kept on nagging
> me to do so. I think it was the right thing
> to do. I hope you agree.
> Is the tour going well? Have you
> met 'him' yet?
> Take care Susie; miss you.
> Love Kath.

Susan put the letter down. I miss you too Kathy she thought. She then wondered what enquiries the police were making. Did they know about the tall thin man, and would they come out to Africa for the tablet?

They were spending three nights in Tamanrasset. Late in the afternoon Susan, Barbara, Johanne and Steve arranged a day's camel trek. They were given the choice of two routes; the mountains or the source. They opted for the source.

Morning came. Eleven of the group were going to take land rovers up to the hermitage at Assekreme, the refuge of Charles de Foucauld. They would stay the night and then rise at dawn to witness the sunrise that was reported to be spectacular in that area of the Hoggar Mountains before returning to camp. The remainder were staying in Tamanrasset.

Susan, Barbara, Johanne and Steve met the guide who was to lead them on the camel trek. He had with him five camels. They each selected a camel and led the beasts a safe distance away from the road. The saddle was in the Touareg style and rested in front of the one hump. A soft cloth covered the saddle, hanging a short way down on either side. The camels crouched down, bending first their front legs and then their back ones. Susan noticed that the saddle had a narrow back and a front part that to her resembled an aircraft's joystick. She positioned herself on the saddle and placed her bare feet on top of the camel's neck. At the guide's command the camels rose. The back legs straightened first, sending Susan lurching forward over the animal's head, and then the front ones. The guide roped the camels one behind the other. Susan was positioned behind the guide and in front of Johanne. They set off on the trek.

Susan thought the ground looked a long way down so hung on tight to the saddle. As time elapsed her confidence grew and she settled into the jolting rhythm of the camel.

'How are you doing Susan?' said a voice from behind.

'Okay thanks Johanne, now that I've got used to it.'

'Have you ridden a camel before?'

'Never. Although I believe I sat on one at the zoo when I was about five, but I don't really remember. How about you?'

'No, first time. Pooh! Your camel is producing the most unpleasant smells.'

'You can say that again' agreed Barbara and Steve.

They progressed at a leisurely pace of about five kilometres an hour. After two hours or so they came to a halt in a small wadi. They dismounted. The guide tied the front legs of each camel in order to stop them from wandering too far. The animals moved away, pausing to chew at the leaves of the acacia trees. Following a cool start the sun, which had at first felt pleasantly warm, was now becoming uncomfortably hot. The guide sat down underneath an acacia and they did likewise.

While they chatted the guide gathered together a few dead twigs and lit a fire. He then made some dough. Once the fire was sufficiently hot he cleared an area in the centre of it into which he placed the dough. This he covered with hot embers and then left it to cook. After thirty minutes he turned the dough over and left it for a further fifteen minutes to finish cooking. Once done he took the round flat loaf from the fire and washed it clean of ash and grit, the heat from within keeping the loaf dry. Susan and the others sampled it with a thin layer of goat butter and together with some tinned sardines they had a delicious lunch. They washed it down with a glass of mint tea which the guide had also made. The meal was finished with a helping of dried dates.

They set off at one thirty and continued to the foot of the mountains and back by an alternative route. The ground was stony causing the camels to stumble but everyone kept their balance. Three and a half hours later they were back at the campsite.

'What a relaxing day' said Susan to Barbara as she dismounted from her camel. 'I've thoroughly enjoyed it.'

'Me too. It was an added bonus to see those Touaregs on their camels just before we arrived back.'

'Did you see they were carrying swords?'

'No I didn't. I suppose I was too intent at looking at their blue robes and their headgear.'

After the evening meal Susan retired to the tent a little earlier than normal. She missed the company of Rebecca and Richard who had both gone to Assekreme.

Susan was awake early. She looked out of the tent just on sunrise. She wondered how it looked in the mountains.

Richard had been up awhile. The sunrise when it came was quite stunning. He wished Susan was there to see it too. He took a couple of photographs.

'Bill, why are we taking a flight to Gao?' asked Matt. 'Why don't we wait for them here in Bamako?'

'Because in Gao we will have the element of surprise. Miss Scarlet will have realised that no one has been following across the desert so therefore won't expect any trouble so far away from the capital city. I have given orders to Karl to meet us there.'

'Let me handle it. I've a score to settle with her.'

'I'll decide upon the course of action. Once I have the tablets then she is yours to do as you please.'

They boarded the aircraft for the internal flight.

Late morning Susan saw the land rovers return from Assekreme. She went over to meet them.

She spotted Rebecca. 'Hi, how was the trip?'

'Okay thanks. The sunrise was good but it was freezing cold when we got up. Did you enjoy the camel trek?'

'Yes. It was a very relaxing day. The camels were okay and the guide cooked some bread in the fire. It was really tasty.'

Richard and Kevin came over to join them.

'Did you have a nice day yesterday?' asked Richard.

'Yes thanks. I was just telling Rebecca how relaxing it was. How about you two?'

'Very enjoyable.'

'Yes it was great' agreed Kevin.

Susan enquired as to whether they were free later in the afternoon and got a yes answer.

'We'll meet at three thirty then' she said 'and Richard, bring your star chart please.'

Three thirty came and the four of them met as planned. They walked a couple of kilometres towards the mountains then rested in the shade of an acacia.

'I've brought the tablets with me. The other night when Richard and I were star gazing I noticed that one of the constellations looked similar to the stars on the second tablet so I thought we might be able to work out which stars are which. There is also something else I want to show you.'

They looked at her in puzzlement but said nothing. She took the tablets from her bag and placed them together.

'What do you see?' she asked.

'Not a lot' answered Rebecca. The others agreed.

'Watch what happens when I put them in the sun.'

She leaned out of the shadow of the acacia tree and placed them in full view of the sun. They watched as the central symbol started to light up.

'Wow. When did you discover that?' asked Rebecca.

'I found out this morning. Look what happens now if I take the second one away.'

She reached across and removed the second tablet. They noticed that the intensity of the symbol reduced by half.

'It must contain a solar cell or something similar' said Kevin.

'Put the other tablet against it please' requested Richard. Susan did so and the symbol doubled in brightness. 'So I wonder what happens when all of the tablets are placed together.'

'I've been thinking about that' answered Susan. 'We know the outer symbols on the central tablet represent the Fibonacci series, so I believe every time you add a tablet the light intensity will go up in the same manner.'

'What Fibonacci series?' asked Kevin looking baffled.

'Sorry Kevin' she said 'I had forgotten you weren't sitting with us when we worked that out back in the pub near Granada.'

She quickly filled him in with the information.

'So you reckon that if we had all six outer tablets the light would shine twenty-one times as brightly.'

'Exactly.'

'That would be a very brilliant beam of light' said Rebecca. 'It's quite bright just with one outer tablet.'

Susan reached over for the tablets.

'Let's have a look at the star chart now please' said Susan looking across to Richard.

'Okay.'

Richard removed the planisphere from his bag. He showed Rebecca and Kevin how it worked then set it down on the ground. Susan turned over the tablets and they compared the stars depicted with the ones on the planisphere.

'I think you are right Susan' said Richard. 'The stars on the second tablet do resemble the stars in the constellation Taurus. You can see the brightest star Aldebaran and the cluster of stars called the Pleiades.' He pointed them out to the others. 'The central tablet seems to include a couple of stars from Taurus and Gemini, however there is a large star featured in the middle that doesn't appear on the chart which is most odd.'

'I suppose it couldn't be a planet like Jupiter' suggested Susan.

'It could be but I somehow doubt it.'

Several minutes passed by and everybody was quiet. Richard was studying the chart. Finally he spoke.

'I have an idea but it seems most unlikely.'

'Tell us then' urged Rebecca.

'Well, the space taken by this large star is nowadays occupied by the Crab Nebula. It is not visible to the naked eye. It is thought that the nebula formed as a result of a supernova some one thousand years ago. So if you were to go back in time there would indeed have been a very bright star there.'

'I wonder when these tablets were made' said Susan.

'And why' added Kevin.

No more notions were forthcoming.

'I need to head back' said Rebecca. 'Are you coming with me Kevin?'

'Sure thing' said Kevin.

They got up and walked in the direction of the campsite. There was an awkward silence which was broken at last by Richard.

'I missed you yesterday. It didn't seem right you not being around.'

'I missed you too' said Susan.

She took hold of Richard's hand and squeezed it. He in turn found the courage to lean across and give her a peck on the cheek.

'Don't stop' urged Susan softly.

This time he kissed her on the lips and Susan reciprocated. It was a long passionate kiss.

Afterwards they sat together holding hands.

'We should be heading back' said Susan looking at her watch.

'I guess so. Come on then.'

They rose and strolled back slowly, happy in each other's company.

That night in the tent Rebecca commented.

'You're happy. I guess my plan must have worked.'

'What plan?'

'Let's say I was following my sixth sense.'

Susan thought for a moment.

'You left us together on purpose didn't you?'

'Of course.'

'Thanks.'

Chapter Thirteen

The group continued on through the Sahara crossing the Tanezrouft, a desolate and inhospitable region of desert, to the Algerian border town of Timiaouine. They then drove to the Malian border town of Tessalit before heading south to the town of Gao situated on the Niger River. The journey from Tamanrasset took six days.

They stayed at a campsite containing a toilet, a bar, a restaurant, some accommodation and a nightly disco. A high brick wall surrounded the compact site. There was only room to pitch one tent and the accommodation was full but it was possible to sleep outside on the mud-brick roof of the disco.

'Hey Bill!'

'Yes Matt, what is it?'

'The truck has arrived. They are staying at the campsite on the edge of town.'

'Excellent. Tomorrow we shall put the plan into operation.'

Bill's attention went back to the packet of biscuits on the table beside him.

Following breakfast the group returned to the centre of town. Their first stop was the bank. It was a slow process but Susan and Rebecca were luckier than most as they were served first. They went outside.

'Do you want a guide?' asked a young boy.

He was about eleven years old. The two girls considered the idea.

'Okay' said Rebecca.

'This way please.'

They followed obediently. Firstly he led them to the markets. These were selling a wide range of foodstuffs plus clothes, cosmetics, jewellery, artefacts and pottery.

'This is great' Rebecca enthused. 'It's nice to see some life after all that time in the desert.'

'I know what you mean.'

Another lad approached with a glass fronted cabinet balanced on his head. Inside was an assortment of rather plain looking cakes.

'Do you fancy a cake?' said Susan.

Rebecca looked at the cakes.

'I don't think so' she answered.

'No thanks' said Susan to the boy.

He left them and headed to another potential customer.

'The cakes didn't look very appetizing and there are too many flies around for my liking' mentioned Rebecca.

They spent a short time looking at the clothes and jewellery.

'Come, I will show you the mosque.'

The lad guided them away from the busy market to a quieter part of town.

'This is the mosque of Kankan Moussa' he declared. 'We can look inside.'

It was a plain, walled, mud brick building. Pipes protruded from it at various places for drainage.

'It's not at all like what I expected' commented Susan.

'Me neither.'

They climbed up to the next level where they had good views of the neighbouring area.

'I take you to the river now' said the boy.

He went downstairs and into the street. They followed but as they exited through the wooden doors they were both seized.

'Keep quiet and come with us then nobody gets hurt' said a voice with a German accent.

The young boy hovered close by, not sure as to what was happening.

'Scram' said a second voice which Susan instantly recognised as that of the tall thin man. The boy fled.

How had he got here Susan wondered. She had been convinced that they had not been followed across the desert.

They were led along a couple of streets passing a few local people on the way who gave them odd looks but otherwise ignored the crazy foreigners. They were led through a wooden gateway into a walled compound. Inside was a large brick building and some mud brick domed huts or outhouses. All seemed deserted. They were led into a room in the large building where a man was sitting at a makeshift table. He was in his fifties, of medium height and build.

'Good, I have been waiting for you to arrive. Now which of you is Miss Scarlet?' asked Bill.

Both girls were silent.

'This one here' said Matt, prodding Susan in the back and making her stumble forwards a little.

'Get rid of the other one please.'

Karl dragged the terrified Rebecca out of the room.

'Leave her alone' said Susan.

'So where is the tablet Miss Scarlet?'

'What tablet?'

'I know you have it so don't waste my time. How did you get it?'

Susan didn't respond.

'Answer him' said Matt who twisted Susan's arm till she yelped.

'My friend gave it to me.'

'And how did she get it?' continued Bill.

'She found it in the park close to where we live.'

'So she didn't buy it then?'

'No.'

'I offered a good price for that tablet. Why do you think that you should have it?'

Susan wasn't sure how to answer. Matt twisted her arm again.

'I don't know' she cried.

'Well I think that I should have it. Now what could be fairer than that?'

'I don't know.'

Karl had re-entered the room.

'And how much did you pay Mr Mansour for his tablet?'

'He - .' Susan realised her mistake immediately but it was too late.

'So you have another tablet as well. How fortunate. Where are they?'

Susan decided it was pointless trying to lie.

'They are in the truck.'

'And where is the truck?'

'I think it returned to the campsite. I'm not sure.'

'It matters not. Karl here will drive you to it. You will get the tablets and return here with them. Then you will both be free to go. You will not speak to anyone unnecessarily. Karl will be watching you at all times. If he suspects anything he will return here and your friend dies. Do you understand me?'

'Yes.'

'Then be on your way.'

Karl grabbed Susan's arm and led her outside and along the street to a parked car.

They drove to the campsite.

The truck was indeed there as she had half expected. Karl watched her every move as she walked through the entrance. There was nobody around from the group. Susan opened up the back of the vehicle, climbed up the steps and went to her locker. After taking out the two tablets, she locked it and left the vehicle, fastening the back steps into position. She was turning to leave when she noticed Alison and Neil sitting having a drink. They waved at her. She wanted to run over and tell them everything but knew it was impossible so waved a reply.

Outside the campsite she got back into the car and was driven back to the compound.

'Where on earth can they have gone?' said Richard looking concerned.

'I don't know' replied Kevin. 'They were only going on a short tour with that young boy. They said they were going to meet us here by the river at ten thirty. It's nearly eleven now.'

'It's not like them to be this late. I hope they aren't in trouble. We will give them five more minutes.'

Bill was munching on some biscuits when Susan entered the room followed closely by Karl.

'Were there any problems?'

'None at all.'

'That is good. Hand me the tablets please Miss Scarlet.'

'Where's my friend?'

'She's fine. Now hand them over.'

'When you release my friend.'

'Did you really think that I would let the two of you go

so that you can tell all and sundry. Now for the last time give me the tablets.'

Susan's fears were realised. She decided to act.

'Here they are.'

She flung her bag directly at Bill, dodged around the surprised Karl and out of the room directly into the path of Matt.

'And where do you think you are going in such a hurry' he said, grabbing hold of her and forcing her back into the room.

The bag had obviously found its target. The biscuits and a glass were no longer on the table but smashed and scattered over the floor. Bill was righting his chair and had hold of her bag.

'Well done Matt. You will pay for that Miss Scarlet' he snarled.

He opened the bag and tipped the contents onto the table. He took hold of the two tablets and brushed the remainder onto the floor. He then opened the pouch he was wearing and took out six more tablets. Seven of the tablets he fitted together while the eighth one he threw at Susan. It fell at her feet.

'That fake one is yours I believe.'

She picked it up.

'Now you will all see the power of this device.'

Chapter Fourteen

'Isn't that the boy who was guiding the girls?' said Kevin pointing across the road.
'Yes, I believe it is' confirmed Richard. 'Come on.'
They hurried over to him.
'Hello. Do you know what happened to the two girls you were guiding?'
The boy seemed reluctant to speak.
'Don't be scared. We want to find our friends. Are they okay?'
The boy contemplated his options for a moment.
'Two men took them away.'
'Took them away?' repeated Richard.
'Yes, as we came out of the mosque.'
'Do you know where they took them?'
'Yes' said the boy.
'Can you guide us there?'
The boy hesitated.
'Yes, okay.'
They set off. The young boy led them to the mosque and then along a further couple of streets.
'The men took them through that gateway.'
'Thanks' said Richard. 'You are a good guide. Here is a little reward.' He pushed some CFA francs into the boy's hand.
'Merci beaucoup monsieur.'
The boy ran off.
'Let us hope they are still here' said Richard.

They walked up to the gate and cautiously opened it. There was nobody about. They entered in silence and made their way across to the large building. A voice could be heard coming from within the building. It sounded like it was speaking in English. They crept quietly inside and made their way towards the room from whence the voice was emanating. They looked inside. Susan stood between two men, one of them they recognised as the tall thin man. Before them another man was speaking. He was threatening Susan. There was no sign of Rebecca.

Kevin pointed at himself and then to the tall thin man. He then pointed at Richard and to the man on Susan's right. Nodding he dashed through the doorway and rugby tackled Matt to the ground. A fraction later Richard had done the same to Karl. In the ensuing struggle Kevin managed to land a right on Matt's jaw while Richard succeeded momentarily in pinning Karl to the ground. Bill decided enough was enough. He calmly took out a gun from his pocket and fired in the air above their heads. The bullet ricocheted off the wall. The fighting ceased.

'Get up all of you.'

They got to their feet. Matt was rubbing his chin. A trickle of blood ran from his mouth.

'Tie these two up and get rid of them.'

'Yes Bill,' said Karl.

He took some string from his pocket and did as he had been ordered. Bill kept the gun pointing at Susan.

Matt and Karl left with the two lads and returned some five minutes later.

'Bring her outside' ordered Bill.

He had put his gun away now and was holding the tablets. They made their way to the quadrangle at the back of the main building.

'Now for a demonstration.'

He angled the tablets, which held together as one quite stably, at the sun. A powerful beam of light was emitted from the central symbol. He aimed it at a piece of dead wood lying on the ground. It instantly ignited.

'Do you see its potential? Maybe I can do another demonstration. Hold her still.'

Matt and Karl gripped each of her arms completely immobilising her. Bill aimed the beam along the ground in Susan's direction producing a line of smoke.

'No, please' she cried.

Before it could reach her a French voice yelled out.

'Arrete maintenant!'

A shot was fired and Bill cried out in pain dropping the tablets which fell to the ground.

'Well if it isn't Michael Williams the art expert' said another voice, this one of English origin. 'What little scheme have you been working on this time?'

Bill was quiet.

'I thought your name was Bill Marks' said Matt in astonishment.

'Oh, this one answers to several names don't you Michael. Take them away please.'

Some commands were issued in French and three Malian policemen walked forward and guided the three men away.

'Are you okay miss?' he asked Susan.

'Yes I'm fine thanks but I don't know what has happened to my three friends.'

The French police officer barked some orders and left with the remaining two Malian policemen.

'So what has been going on here?'

Susan gave a short précis of all that had occurred and

walked across to the tablets which were on the ground. She picked them up and passed them to him.

'What brought you here?' she asked.

'I believe you know a girl called Kathy Rand.'

'Yes. I share a flat with her back in London.'

'Well, she told us about the tablet that she had found and had passed on to you. She also gave us a good description of Matt. He has a record and we eventually traced his whereabouts. While searching his flat we found a crumpled packet of tobacco. It was Moroccan. It established an African connection. It wasn't much of a lead but the only one we had. Further checks with the border agencies concerning him led us here.'

There were footsteps and Rebecca, Richard and Kevin appeared with the French officer.

'Oh thank god you are all okay' said Susan running to them.

'Susie' said Rebecca, tears of happiness streaming down her face. She gave her friend a big hug. 'I didn't think I was going to see you again.'

'Thanks all of you' Susan said, giving Kevin a hug and then kissing Richard.

'How come I don't get a kiss' commented Kevin smiling.

'I'll tell you later' said Rebecca.

'We will need to take a statement from you at the police station' said the English police officer to Susan.

'Did you book the river trip for this afternoon Richard?' asked Susan.

'Yes. It departs at one.'

Susan looked at her watch. It was half past twelve.

She turned to the police officer.

'Can the statement wait till later please? We have time to catch the boat if we hurry and it would be a shame to miss it after coming all this way.'

'I see no reason why not. I will get a man to meet you at the end of your excursion.'

'Many thanks.' She turned to the others. 'Shall we gather our stuff together and go on the trip?'

'If you're up to it then I am' agreed Rebecca.

'Sure thing.'

'Let's go then' urged Richard.

Chapter Fifteen

It was Thursday the 2nd of April.

'There she is' said Kathy to Barry as they waited for the arrivals of the flight from Amsterdam to come through immigration. 'Susie, over here.'

Susan heard a familiar voice call her name. It was Kathy. She ran over as best as she could, dropped her bag, and gave Kathy a big hug.

'Hi Kath. It's so lovely to see you. I didn't know you were coming to the airport.'

'I hadn't planned to but as Barry here wasn't working we decided to drive over.' Barry introduced himself. 'So where is he?'

Rebecca, Richard and Kevin came up and joined them. Susan introduced them to Kathy and Barry.

'Do you know Susan only went on the tour to find a man' remarked Kathy grinning.

Both Susan and Richard went red.

'I am going to kill you when I get home' said Susan grinning also.

'What happened to the tablets?'

'The police officer took them although I do have one as a souvenir.'

'Oh yes, the fake one, you mentioned that in your letter.'

'Yes' agreed Susan.

She didn't tell Kathy and she hadn't told the others that she had in fact still got the central tablet. She had switched it with the fake when she had handed them over. It was too powerful a device, she reasoned, to keep all of the pieces together, as she had so nearly found out. She wanted to discover the real purpose why it had been made. For the time being it would remain her secret. Anyhow, one of the tablets did legally belong to her, the one Mr Mansour had given her, and she had high hopes that his piece would be returned to her by the police in due course. She would write to Mr Mansour at the earliest opportunity.

Lightning Source UK Ltd.
Milton Keynes UK
UKOW02f1603140415

249620UK00002B/27/P